When she stepped up onto her stairs and turned to face him the way she looked at his mouth for long seconds before looking him in the eye was invitation enough. He hadn't waited for her the past ten years, but she'd always remained the ideal.

He slipped his arms around her waist and closed his mouth over hers, kissing her with the longing he'd never lost.

Her soft lips parted in an instant, not only welcoming his tongue into her mouth but inviting. As natural as breath—and as needed.

The hands on his back squeezed, fingers pressing into his flesh in a way that caused a riot of goosebumps and driving chills under the now dry material. No one else tasted like Jolie. No one else kissed like her either. She'd hold the kiss as long as he did—oxygen be damned.

When his heart had sped up to the point that he needed air he broke the kiss, but kept her close enough for them to fight for the same air with big, shuddering breaths.

"This is a bad idea," Jolie whispered, swallowing and licking her kiss-swelled lips.

Reece shook his head. "Good idea."

"Bad idea. Bad, bad…"

She kissed him this time, releasing her hold on him to get at her jacket buttons and shed the bulky material that kept them further apart. Freed from it, she pressed tight against him, the gauzy material of her dress leaving very little to his vivid imagination. God, he wanted to feel her. *Everywhere.*

Dear Reader

I'd love to open this letter with something deep and philosophical that inspired me to write RETURN OF DR IRRESISTIBLE... Or I could go on at length about my fascination with the circus micro-culture, and how it doesn't matter because at heart people are people...

But really...? I just wanted to write about the circus! Who *doesn't* like the circus?

My motivation was really that deep at the start. So, naturally, as I had no vested interest in the subject at the outset, writing the book provided me with insights into my own psyche. I should expect that to happen by now, but it's always a surprise when it does.

It doesn't matter if you grew up in the suburbs, in a circus, or in the hills of Appalachia: everyone feels like a weirdo or an outsider at some point. And you always have to step outside your safe zone to grow past that.

Take risks. Be brave. And for the love of chocolate and fat, and roly-poly puppies, go to the circus whenever you can! :)

Amalie xo

www.amalieberlin.com
Twitter: @AmalieBerlin
Facebook: www.facebook.com/amalie.berlin

RETURN OF
DR IRRESISTIBLE

BY
AMALIE BERLIN

First published in Great Britain 2014
by Mills & Boon, an imprint of Harlequin (UK) Limited,
Eton House, 18-24 Paradise Road, Richmond, Surrey, TW9 1SR

© 2014 Amalie Berlin

ISBN: 978-0-263-24389-5

Harlequin (UK) Limited's policy is to use papers that are natural,
rene͟   ͟n in
sust͟   ͟conform
to th

Prin
by C

There's never been a day when there haven't been stories in **Amalie Berlin**'s head. When she was a child they were called daydreams, and she was supposed to stop having them and pay attention. Now when someone interrupts her daydreams to ask, 'What are you doing?' she delights in answering, 'I'm working!'

Amalie lives in Southern Ohio with her family and a passel of critters. When *not* working she reads, watches movies, geeks out over documentaries and randomly decides to learn antiquated skills. In case of zombie apocalypse she'll still have bread, lacy underthings, granulated sugar, and always something new to read.

Recent titles by Amalie Berlin:

UNCOVERING HER SECRETS
CRAVING HER ROUGH DIAMOND DOC

**These books are also available in eBook format
from www.millsandboon.co.uk**

Dedication

To my little brother Seth, a great writer whose name
will be on the front of a book before long. He who
read my first book (even though it's a romance) and
promotes my new releases to the point that my secret
identity is no longer secret with my family (doh!).
If I end up on the prayer chain for acts of
text-based naughtiness it's all his fault.

To my editor, Laurie Johnson. She's either very brave
or she's got a heck of a poker face. This was our first
book together and she didn't even hesitate when I
emailed to let her know: 'I WANT TO WRITE A
MEDICAL ROMANCE SET AT THE CIRCUS!
YAY!' Nerves. Of. Steel.

CHAPTER ONE

FOR TEN YEARS Dr. Reece Keightly had been dreading this night.

He'd known it would come to this. Of course he'd known. It was all on his shoulders—the dynasty, the future of the company and the weight of the past. Two centuries of history all ending with him.

The tenth-generation owner of Keightly Circus was the one who would tear it all down. Nice round number, ten. Like Fate had decreed it. Like he was just filling the role assigned to him. Like it wasn't his fault.

Except it was. That's how they'd see it.

Reece took a step forward, shuffling with the crowded line to the ticket booth. The traditional last annual stop of the circus was always Atlanta due to its proximity to where they summered, but it was also the best crowd. The local, hometown circus returning triumphant from a season on the road, played out the last week near home. Traditional, like so many other things with his family's circus. Keightly's prided themselves on tradition.

Due to the coverage given to the impending closing—local television and radio stations had blared the news for weeks—they were enjoying record crowds for the last performances. For Atlantans, parents had been coming with their children for generations. Another tradition that would be violated after this year.

As excited as he was to see the show—and he never lost that excitement—the prospect of seeing people he cared for putting their lives in danger built in him a kind of extreme awareness of the world around him. It slowed things down, pulled him out of himself, and amplified every ounce of fear until it became a physical sensation, the taste of cold metal on the back of his tongue and he couldn't swallow past it.

Excited terror. He almost longed for ignorance, to be just one of the crowd, another random person in line who only knew the fantasy. But Reece knew the horror too.

All around him children giggled and chattered happily. Ahead, inside the massive blue tent, the band tuned up, readying to start the show, and every note amplified the dread eating at him. The sawdust awaited him. A tradition he could do without.

Dwelling on the unpleasant details wouldn't help him deal with them better. Shut it down. He just needed to see this show. One last time, make certain he was making the right decision. Not that he had any real doubts, but two hundred years deserved one last think. One last chance for them to change his mind.

Two people away from the ticket counter, he heard the first slow whistles of the calliope wheezing through the lot. Soon the ancient steam-powered contraption blanketed the area in sound—cheerful music silenced his chaotic thoughts.

He'd always loved the old calliope, but in the wake of those first warbling notes a surge of homesickness slammed into him. Nostalgia so strong it was like overlapping two realities—belonging and alienation, comfort and terror, peace and anger.

He latched on to the last emotion. Anger was better. He could do this—be angry enough to drown out the rest. But he should at least be honest with himself—he wanted to be there if for no other reason than to see her perform. He wanted to see them all, but the promise of Jolie Bohannon in the spotlight would see him through.

He just needed to see the show one more time. Everything would be fine.

Say goodbye.

Purge the sawdust from his blood, and all the rest of it.

One last time.

Then he'd take care of everyone. See them settled. And go back to his safe and orderly life. Find a place to build his practice. Buy a home with a foundation beneath it. He could have people relying on him for their health—it's what he'd been raised to do—but not while he had to stand by and watch them put their lives in jeopardy to make people cheer.

Out of the corner of his eye he caught his first glimpse of the steam-powered calliope rolling across the lot. His mother sat at the back, playing the piano-like keyboard that operated the old steam whistles, while Mack Bohannon drove the carriage.

Jolie's family had traveled with Keightly Circus since before the Civil War. They might as well be family for real, and soon there would be a link when his mother married Mack and left Reece as the last Keightly standing.

Not yet ready to be seen, Reece pulled down the brim of his fedora, hunching his shoulders like that would make him stand out less. Keightly men grew tall. Every one well over six feet. But nobody expected him to be here tonight, and he didn't know how they'd react to his presence. He wanted to just be an observer.

He had a right to be angry. Reece harbored no illusions, though—if this were a movie, he'd be wearing black and twirling a weird mustache in the corner. Only villains closed circuses… Even if he was making the right call for the right reasons, something beloved was dying. Making the death of the circus quick rather than letting it limp along on life support was a kindness.

If he wasn't going to take the reins, if he wasn't going to step up as the last Keightly and lead, he had to take care of laying the show to rest. And he would do that. With the respect and honor it deserved.

But first he'd see one last show and say goodbye on his own.

And maybe somewhere along the way he'd find a way of convincing himself he wasn't a monster.

Jolie Bohannon stood at the back of the tent, holding Gordy's leash. The miniature white stallion always had to be held back until it was absolutely time for him to enter the ring. He lived to perform, a feeling she could once have identified with. It was still there—in theory—but she had other important responsibilities to handle now. Like making sure the full-sized mounts and the Bohannon Trick-riders didn't accidentally trample Gordy because someone let him off his leash too soon. Calm and orderly, that's how everything and everyone stayed safe.

She listened for the change in the music—everyone in the circus learned to gauge where the performance was by the music—and adjusted Gordy's flashy silver bridle and the wee matching and no less flashy saddle. His costume.

At the first trumpet, she unclipped his harness and reached for the tent flap, barely getting her hand in before he barreled through the flap and down the causeway. She stepped through in time to see him enter the ring. Darting between the other horses ridden by the Bohannon Trick-riders, he stopped dead center, reared on his back legs to stretch to his tallest—four feet and some change—and whinnied.

One by one, the other horses in the ring bowed to him,

the little king. The little clown to end the act, the segment of the horse act that reached out to the children and in the audience, drew them in, and got their minds away from the scary excitement of moments before. Jolie smiled. Gordy could still make her smile.

The show was almost over. One more act and then the finale.

She stepped back outside, listening and watching the bustle of the crew getting ready to change the ring for the next act.

Watching the show was a little too much for her right now. She never let her emotions get out of control. Never. But with the circus closing down for good, emotions she'd long ago buried seemed closer to the surface. The last thing she needed was for something to set her off. Watching the show, getting sentimental and weepy over the last performances? Would interfere with her job. Everyone had a job to do and they'd do it with or without her, but she had to hold up her end. That meant right now she had to stand here and wait while Gordy played the fool and the crew changed the set, but she didn't have to watch the well-oiled machine.

The music stopped suddenly, snapping Jolie's attention back to the present. In a well-oiled machine, the music never stopped for no reason.

A cold feeling crept up over the back of her head. That emotion could never be buried or ignored. But fear could be used.

Cries had barely begun rising from the crowd before Jolie was inside the tent, running toward the ring. There she found her family off their mounts, surrounding something.

Where was Gordy?

She burrowed through and found him lying on his side, all playfulness gone. He thrashed about, repeatedly trying and failing to rise. She didn't have to look hard to see that his front left leg was injured. Not again.

Three of her cousins stepped in to try and get him to his feet, but he bit at them.

"Get out of the way. Call a vet. We need a vet." Her order was loud enough to be heard above the din. Gordy was her responsibility. Her job... But more than that, she loved him. He depended on her to take care of him.

Grabbing her phone from her pocket, she thrust it at her uncle as she moved past, holding on to her calm. Gordy needed orderliness and calm from her. "Whoa, Gordy. It's okay. Whoa..."

He was just scared and in pain. She squatted at his side and, despite his thrashing, got the straps circling his belly unbuckled and the spangled saddle off. Freeing him from the extra weight didn't help him rise on his own, and she needed to see him on his feet.

He wouldn't bite her. He'd never bitten her.

Taking a breath, she leaned in, arms surging for his chest and belly to try and help the small stallion to his feet.

"Jolie, his leg is broken." She heard a deep man's voice, winded but loud. Someone who'd been running too, familiar and unfamiliar even if he said her name. Too busy to question it further, she tried again to lift Gordy. So heavy. Jolie adjusted her arms and tried harder, straining to get the tiny stallion off the ground without putting any pressure on that leg.

He got on his knees, but she wasn't strong enough to get him all the way up. The position put pressure put on his leg and her favorite friend peeled his lips back and bit into her forearm. The shock of the bite hit her almost as sharply as the pain radiating up her arm.

She must have hurt him because it wasn't a quick bite. His jaw clenched and ground slightly, like he was holding back something intent on hurting him. He held on, and so did Jolie.

Someone stepped to the other side of the horse and put his arms around Gordy's middle. "On three." She gritted her teeth, counted, and the excessively large man lifted with her.

This time Gordy's back legs came under him and they got him to his feet, or least to the three good ones. She needed to see him standing, assess how bad the break was. It occurred to her that she should be more freaked out about this.

Veterinary medicine had come a long way since the days when a broken leg had been a death sentence for a horse, but Gordy may as well be living in the Wild West. He had a history of leg problems. Jolie remembered what they'd gone through the last time and what Gordy had gone through. Someone would make that terrible suggestion. Someone would say they should put him down… She needed to keep that from happening.

She also really needed him to stop biting. A few deep breaths and she'd be able to control the pain, but it'd be easier if he'd let go. Having her screaming at him would freak the tiny horse out and he was already afraid.

"Let go now," the man said, pulling her attention back to him over Gordy's pristine white back. She expected to see a vet, or maybe someone who had traveled with the circus in the past…

Ten years had changed his face. Broadened it. Made it more angular. But she knew those eyes—the boy she'd known ten years ago. The boy she'd loved.

Reece wasn't supposed to be there yet. And he probably wasn't supposed to be looking like he was about to throw up.

"I can't let go." Jolie grunted. Speaking took effort. Suddenly everything took effort. Controlling the pain.

Controlling her voice. Breathing… "He's got me." And letting go might just mean that he fell again, hurt himself worse, and maybe his teeth would take her flesh with him.

As much as Jolie might normally appreciate the value of distraction to help her control wayward emotions, Reece was the wrong kind of distraction. He just added a new dimension of badness to the waves racing up her arm. She didn't want him there. He wasn't supposed to come until they were all on the farm, where she'd have room to avoid him. He'd stayed gone for ten years so why in the world would he come to see the show now?

Because she didn't want it. But here he was, helping with Gordy and being gigantic. Good lord, he was big.

She could use that to help Gordy.

Get the horse and the show back on their feet.

The throng of people gathered around, children in the audience pressed against the raised outside of the ring, getting as close as they could… The weight of all their emotions pressed into her.

It had to be their emotions she was feeling. She'd mastered her own emotions several years ago, and maintained proper distance from anything hairy, she reminded herself. And she'd regain control of them as soon as she got Gordy out of there and Reece the hell away from her.

First things first. "We have to get him out of here." She needed out of there too.

A single nod and Reece reached for the horse's mouth while she kept him standing. Large, strong hands curled around the snout and lower jaw and he firmly pried the miniature horse's jaws apart, all the while speaking to him gently, making comforting sounds that did nothing to comfort her—but which seemed to do the trick with Gordy.

Or the combination of comfort and brute strength did the trick. Gordy released her bleeding arm and immediately Reece slid his arms under the horse's neck and through his legs to support his chest and hind quarters. Then he did what she'd never seen anyone do before: He picked the horse up.

"Which way?" Strained voice to go with strained muscles, and the look of nausea was still on his face. How had Reece gotten so strong? She thought doctors studied all the time and played golf... Even as small as Gordy was, he was still a horse and weighed a good one hundred and eighty pounds. But Reece carried the miniature horse out of the ring. By himself.

Right. Not the time to think about that. Gordy was hurt. She was hurt. The show had stopped. Children were probably very scared and upset. "This way." She cleared a path and led Reece and his load out the back of the tent, the way she'd come, off toward the stables.

He could carry Gordy to the stable and then go away, let her have her mind back. The stable was Bohannon property, she would just order him out and take care of her horse.

Someone else would step in, get the show moving again, and she didn't care who that task fell to. As long as the vet came soon.

The stable wasn't far, but by the time they reached it, Reece was breathing hard. Maybe harder than she was while desperately trying not to feel nothing—not the pain in her arm, and really not the anger and betrayal bubbling up from that dark place she stuffed all her Reece emotions.

Once in Gordy's stall with the fresh hay she'd put down earlier, Jolie directed, "Lay him in the straw." That was something she could think to say. One step at a time, that's as far ahead as she could make her mind work. It took more effort than it might have otherwise done if she hadn't been bitten and her arm didn't ache to the point she was considering that maybe the bone had fractured...

The rest of her mental capacity was filled to the brim with the echoes of voices reminding her of Gordy's history, the way Mack would undoubtedly react, and all the animals she'd lost over the years. Of everything she'd lost…

Ignoring those voices took effort.

Nothing was going to happen to Gordy. He was practically a sibling. Her first mount when she'd been little more than a toddler herself.

Jolie forced herself to still. Reece gently laid the injured but considerably calmer animal in the bedding. "I think he remembers you," she murmured. Gordy remembered Reece, even if he looked loads different—even if he'd bitten *her*. He remembered Reece enough to go docilely into the straw.

Still not a good enough reason to keep Reece in the stable. She couldn't focus with him there. "Thank you. Go watch the rest of the show." She got in between him and the horse, focusing with all her might on first-aid training for horses.

Reece stood behind her, looking down over her shoulder. "Let me look at your arm."

"It will wait." Gordy might have thrashed himself into a bad intestinal situation…so the next step should be…

Reece's hands closed around her waist, dragging her attention away from what she should be doing. He lifted her to her feet and secured her left arm with his horse-lifting grip locked around her wrist. Fire and ice, his touch was like peppermint, an utterly inexplicable combination of heat and chill that momentarily cut through the fear of losing Gordy and made her think…so many different things. Primarily it reminded her of one thing: He needed to leave. But Gordy needed to stand up more, and she'd failed at lifting him to his feet twice already.

"My arm can wait," she repeated. And it could wait

outside his grasp. She twisted her wrist free, ignored the deep ache the motion caused, and pointed to Gordy. "He needs to be on his feet."

"He can rest a moment. You're hurt."

He sounded so sincere, genuinely concerned... Which was crap, of course. "He needs to be on his feet," she repeated, "Resting a moment is the last thing he needs." *Don't look him in the eyes. Don't look him in the eyes.*

"Jolie..."

"Reece..." she replied, and looked him in the eyes. Right. No time to waste. She started moving again, toward the stall door so she could get to the supplies and away from him. Something in his touch, in the fact that he had helped them, and the concern in his eyes made her feel weak, muddied her thinking. Roused emotions she couldn't afford right now.

She knew what needed to happen for Gordy, not him. "You can stay here until I get him in a sling. He needs to be in a sling. And don't think you get to tell me what to do just because you went all strongman and carried my horse to the stable. You don't get to dictate anything in here. The circus might be yours to destroy, but Gordy is a Bohannon, so I'll take your help with him, and then you can get the hell out of my stable."

Not calm. Not calm at all. What had happened to her calm? Her arm. Pain and fear did this to her. That and the weirdness of seeing Reece. But it would all go away again soon enough. Losing Gordy on top of everything else would be a pain she couldn't ignore. Sling. She needed one of the horse slings.

Flipping open the lid of the trunk where various first-aid implements were kept, Jolie dug through, using her injured arm even if every second the ache grew worse. The only sling she knew they had was for the big horses...

"Tell me what you're doing." Reece said, apparently deciding it wasn't worth fighting with her.

Good. She didn't have time to fight.

Reece moved to the side of the trunk. "I'll help you if you tell me what you need."

More Good. Be helpful. The sooner Gordy was on his feet, the sooner Reece could go away. "I didn't see him fall," she said. "I don't know how much he could have jarred his insides when he went down, but I saw him thrashing to get up and that could have twisted his bowel. I don't want him fighting colic while his body needs to be focused on healing his leg. We need a sling. And some way to hang it. I'll work on the sling, you see if you can find a couple of pieces of lumber that will stretch across the top of the stall."

He left immediately. Of course he knew the way. The circus might be somewhere new every week, but it was always set up in the same layout. And that layout hadn't changed in the last ten years. She'd changed. He'd changed—God, had he ever—but the circus was the same.

A few minutes later Reece came back with two especially thick posts thrown over one shoulder and found her crouched in Gordy's stall, stringing together belts and harnesses.

"Lay them across the top. This isn't a proper sling, but it should work until the vet gets here." She stretched the leather across Gordy's chest, noting the labored breathing, and fought down another wave of panic. Once she had it in place over the shoulder she could access, she looked at Reece. "Think you can pick him up again? I need to get this around the other side and I need him on his feet, so I need you just supporting that place where his leg is compromised. Then I'll climb the stall and get it all hitched to the lumber."

He scowled at her. What did that mean? A longer look

at her arm told her why he looked so sour, but to his credit he squatted beside Gordy and got him up again, just as she'd asked. Which didn't make up for anything. He would probably pitch some kind of fit when this was over. He was a showman after all. Doctor. Showman. Jerkface.

She'd been upset with him for years, but had thought she'd finally let go of it a few years ago. The strength of her anger at seeing him now surprised her.

Not that she could spare time for reflection. To hell with Reece. She'd help Gordy—they'd help him. He'd survive. Get him up. Get the vet to cast his leg. Take care of him. Not a detailed plan, but it was as good as she had right now. And when Gordy's leg was in a cast, she'd figure out what the next step was. And then the next. She had a job, and right now Gordy was it.

"Hurry..." Reece said through clamped lips, doing his best to keep his head away from Gordy's mouth, should he get bitey again, but he managed to get the little stallion on his hooves and support his chest.

Jolie ducked around the other side and in a few seconds had threaded the makeshift harness through, clipped the ends together and thrown the long tail up and over the wood.

Good thing they were all pretty much acrobats...and that she was good at jumping. Her small stature made her the perfect size for tossing and flying, but made reaching objects in tall cabinets or shelves difficult. Made hauling herself to the stall top require a hop first.

She grabbed the top of the stall with both hands. Pain shot up her left arm and she let go again. It took a few seconds for the buzzing to subside so she could try again.

"Jolie?"

"I'm okay. It's...probably not broken."

He swore under his breath. Like he cared that much. Like someone who'd cut those he'd supposedly loved out of his life for a decade could care at all, let alone enough to swear.

A burst of anger at the bitter memory gave her the strength she needed to pull herself up on the second attempt. She maneuvered herself between the lumber Reece had slatted across the top of the stall, balanced and reached for the leather dangling over the lumber.

As she worked, she looked down and saw Reece scowling up at her again. "What?"

"Hurry," he said.

"You carried him all the way in there, is supporting one end such a chore now?" She looked down, noticed red on Gordy's white fur and howled, "Is he bleeding?"

"Dammit, Jolie, that's *your* blood."

"Oh." She swallowed back down another wave of hysteria and fastened the belts until the little horse was lifted ever so slightly from the floor.

"Too high," he called. "His front hooves aren't on the ground."

"I think the next notch will put too much weight on his leg, though... This is the best we can do. Maybe we can find a tile or bit of wood, something to slide under his good foot so he can stand but keep the weight off the other."

"After we clean your arm."

Back to the arm. "Later. What happened out there? You saw it, right?" Should she give him a sedative? Could she even do the math right now to figure out the right dose, or find a vein to inject it?

"He hurdled a little leap and just landed badly." He let go of Gordy slowly, letting him test the sling, and she waited to climb down until she was certain she wouldn't have to adjust the buckles.

Reece got to that decision before she did then stood and plucked her off the top of the stall. Picking her up again.

She'd forgotten he did that, just picked her up whenever he wanted to. And now that he was twelve gazillion feet tall, he might be even worse about it.

"Good grief, put me down." Being this close to him made her feel more breathless than she wanted to sound. She wanted to sound angry. Angry was better than fragile and girly.

"I'm helping you down."

She couldn't kick him because he might drop her and she already hurt. Though in a way she was grateful for the pain as having something else to focus on had to help keep her from thinking too hard about the past and just what Reece was there to do. "I climbed up on my own, I could've climbed down without your help too."

"You're hurt, and you're too stubborn to let me take care of you...your wound." He set her in the straw, and when Gordy whinnied and tugged at the sling, he lowered his voice. "It needs to be cleaned at the very least. Animal mouths..."

"I know. But it's waited this long. If I'm going to catch some dreaded horse-bite disease, then I'm pretty sure there is no difference in waiting fifteen minutes to clean it or fifty."

Gordy thrashed about, trying to escape the makeshift sling, causing the lumber above to skid on the stall. Jolie watched the wood move enough to be convinced: Gordy definitely needed a tranquilizer. And she needed a shot of something too. Like whiskey.

"Who's going to take care of him if you're sick?"

"I won't get sick. You're the one who's been looking like you were going to throw up."

He ignored her vomit talk. "This is ridiculous. He is in the sling. There is absolutely nothing else you can do for him until the vet arrives. Come with me to Mom's RV and let me treat it."

"No." She redirected his attention. "I have some sedative but I need some help with the math. You do medicine dosage calculations all the time, right?"

"I don't know the dosage for horses," Reece muttered, but reached up to hold the lumber steady.

"I know the dosage for a big horse and the weight differences, so you should be able to figure out what to give Gordy if I tell you that, right?"

"Fine, then we'll deal with your arm." He looked at her, but direct eye contact did something to her insides and she had enough to worry about.

She looked away, told him the dosage for a full-sized horse and the weight differences, and then left him thinking and holding the lumber to run to her trailer where she had the medication in her fridge. When she came back, he stood there still and immediately told her the number.

Flipping the cap back on the needle, she plunged it into the vial and extracted a slightly smaller amount than Reece had told her. Just to be safe. "You can treat my arm when the vet gets here. Gordy needs me. He needs reassurance. The last thing he needs is to be alone and scared."

"Jolivetta Chriselle Ra—"

"You just stop right there, Dr. Reece I'm-Going-To-Act-Like-The-Boss Keightly." She'd poke him in the chest if her arm didn't hurt so much and she didn't have a needle in the other. "I'm not going anywhere. The vet or someone might come in and get the idea of putting him down if I'm not here to stop them. Now, let go of the wood and hold him still. This medicine isn't great in the muscle—it eats it up. Has to go into the vein."

"Do you want me to do it?" Reece asked. Like she hadn't done this a hundred times before.

"No. I want you to hold Gordy." *And stop being bossy. And stop being around. And stop being...everything else.*

Reece let go of the wood, rubbed a hand over his face

like he could wipe off frustration, and slung his arms around Gordy's chest again, his voice gentling a little too. "Why are you so convinced they're going to put him down?"

"He's got leg problems."

"Explain."

"Really bad circulation." Jolie maneuvered to the other side of the horse before adding, "And he's broken that leg before. It was very hard to heal the first time…"

"So it might be kinder if they come to that decision now rather than after—"

"No!" She shouted, causing the horse to flinch. She took a breath and calmed her voice. "It's not going to come to that. Horses can survive broken legs. And the circus is closing anyway! He has time to recuperate."

She went for a vein she had found before, back of the neck, easier to get to and somewhere where she could talk softly and provide comfort. Not that she felt calm and comforting right now. She felt way too much of everything. Worry. Fear. Betrayal. Anger. A disconcerting awareness at Reece's foreign manly scent in the stable… But she channeled worry away for Gordy's benefit and gentled her tone. "We're leaving here and going back to the farm in a few days, and he'll have space to relax and get better. He doesn't need to get better fast so that he can perform."

"It's nothing to do with performing."

"No, it's about taking the easy way out. Gordy's part of the family, and you don't just shoot your family if they get a hangnail." She threaded the needle into the vein, pulled back to make sure blood came into the cartridge, and then injected slowly. "You take care of your family. At least, that's how it's done in my family. You might not be willing to fight for yours, but I am."

The sedation worked almost instantly. She hadn't given Gordy enough to knock him out, but he did stop thrashing and mellowed significantly. With the safety cap back in place, she waved Reece off Gordy's back. "You can go now."

"You know no one is going to put him down if he has a chance to recover." He moved to the door of the stall but didn't leave. "I'm not leaving until you stop acting like a crazy woman and let me get a look at your arm."

If he didn't stop going on about her arm and about Gordy's leg, she might hit him. From the angle she'd have to swing up to hit his chin, and might even be able to knock him out. Providing his jaw was more glass than the granite it looked like. "He has a chance."

"Just wait for the vet." Reece leaned against the jamb.

She slid past him to grab a stool and moved it back into the stall. "I have been taking care of horses forever." Okay, she might be acting crazy—she'd never felt moved to violence before—but Gordy was important. "And I take care of people too. I know what I'm talking about. He can be casted. Sometimes a kind of exoskeleton can be built to support a broken leg. I've read about it, and we have the slings for the big horses. We have one who has a metabolic condition that causes him to get laminitis, and we had to sling him once. This little makeshift sling is taking weight off that leg, and we can get a better one for him set up. It's temporary. So stop preparing me for the worst."

Her throbbing arm needed a break, and so did she. She scooted the stool toward Gordy's head with her feet. He might be sedated but he'd feel her there. She'd comfort him. And maybe she'd absorb a little comfort from keeping near him too. A little comfort would be good right now. "I hope you're not so fast on the plug-pulling for your *people* patients."

CHAPTER TWO

REECE RUBBED HIS HEAD, a headache starting between his brows. This was not how he'd pictured their reunion going. That had gone entirely differently. She'd been wearing something sparkly for starters.

"Hey…" His brain caught up with the situation now that the immediate emergency had passed. "You're not dressed."

"I'm dressed just fine," she bit at him, and then her voice turned honey-sweet as she began to pet Gordy's face and talk to him. "It's going to be okay. I won't let anyone hurt you."

"For the show," he cut in. He'd been waiting at the show the whole time to see her perform, and only now did it register with him that she wasn't dressed for the ring at all. Jeans and a pink T-shirt with a white unicorn and a rainbow coming from its butt, while funny, wasn't performance attire. "You haven't performed yet. I figured you'd come at the end, the aerial act maybe, but you're not dressed."

"I don't perform any more."

"Why not?"

"None of your business." Her words were angry, but she kept her tone sweet. Not for him, he realized. She looked back at Gordy and ruffled his ears. The sedative had taken the fight out of the little horse, but her touch and proximity soothed him. Despite the drug, he tilted his head against hers and accepted the comfort.

She had the touch. Reece forgot his irritation for a few seconds, remembering the way she'd sat with his head in her lap after the accident, petting his temples in much the same way she that she petted the horse's face now too.

Two people in one body. In the ring she came alive—so full of energy that even when a trick failed she still held the audience in her hands. And the rest of the time she had that gentle touch that soothed any kind of animal. Even teenage boys. She'd been the only one he'd wanted around him after Dad had died.

The pink T-shirt had a growing spot of red on it where she'd clamped her arm to her side, cradling it protectively against her and using her other arm for Gordy.

"Hurts?"

"Adrenalin is wearing off," she murmured, "but I can wait."

"No doubt." He made a note to ask Mom all the things about Jolie that he'd never let her tell him before, when he had been trying so hard to stay in school and keep Jolie off his mind. Something was up with her, and it wasn't just upset about Gordy's accident. It might even be about more than his reason for being there, and the myriad other reasons she had to be angry with him. Not performing any more wasn't something she'd have decided for the last week of the circus. It was older than his decision to close the show down. How much older, he had no idea.

He was saved from thinking further about what kind of knots Jolie might have worked herself into while he'd been away when Mack Bohannon escorted the vet into the stable and ushered Reece and Jolie out—two too many people for the small stall.

"I know that's not a proper sling." Jolie said, gesturing to the small injured horse from the gate, "but I couldn't think of anything else we could do for him that might keep his digestion working properly and keep weight off that leg. We don't have a sling small enough for him."

"I have one." The vet pulled a backpack off his shoulder and handed it to Mack, Jolie's uncle and head of the Bohannon clan. Ultimately, Gordy's future rested with Mack, who dug into the pack and retrieved the sling then proceeded to help the vet swap it with the makeshift one.

"He's going to be okay. He can heal this," Jolie said to Mack, who looked grim. Not the right look. Not one Reece wanted to see any more than Jolie did. Whatever her protestations, she didn't need to watch the play-by-play.

He reached for her shoulder and tried to pivot her toward the door. "Let's get your arm tended to."

"I'm not leaving yet." Mack looked back at her and she shook her head, her chin lifting, "I'm not leaving. You might need me."

As easy as he'd like to be with Jolie of all people, he'd mistakenly thought perhaps time would have made her somewhat less stubborn. She'd always been this way when it came to Gordy, and Reece had started throwing his weight around to get her to mind him all those years ago when her mother had gotten her back when she'd been taken. That had been the first time his father had ever put him in charge of anyone in the company.

She thought him bossy? Well, she made him bossy.

The vet needed room to work and, knowing very well how hard it was to treat a patient when being hovered over, Reece made his decision. He scooped her legs from under her as his other arm caught across her back, and he carried her out of the stable.

Too stunned to say anything for a few seconds, it took them actually leaving the stables for Jolie's indignation and terror to kick back in. "Reece! Reece, put me down. I need to stay with Gordy."

"You need your arm cleaned and inspected." Reece tightened his arms lest she take a mind to thrash free of his grip. "I'm done talking about it. Mom will have first-aid supplies in her RV."

"No. What if they decide to put him down while I'm gone? He needs an advocate. He needs me there to promise to take care of him. See him through this again. I know he can heal." She twisted, testing his hold, and then locked onto him with a baleful glare. "Please." The word didn't go well with the glare or the tone.

"It won't take long."

"It will take five minutes to walk to your mom's RV. If you must have your way, my trailer is closer!" As the words tumbled out, she realized what would convince him. "I have all the medical supplies anyway, I'm the EMT on staff. And I won't fight you if you go there and we do this fast. Or just let me go do it myself and—"

"You're an EMT?" He stopped walking and looked down at her, his eyes going from hers to her mouth long enough to distract her. Kissing...would be bad.

Don't look at his mouth. "Can't you walk and talk at the same time?" Jolie barked at him, startling his gaze back to hers. "I am an EMT, yes." With the stable now officially out of sight, the firm heat of his big body and the prospect of being alone with Reece began to scare her more than Gordy's plight. One crisis at a time, that's all she could deal with. Not knowing what she might say or how she might react when she got her emotions sorted out? Well, that could cause another crisis. "Put me down and let me clean it myself, or start walking. Don't just stand here while they might be making decisions without me!"

"Didn't you have to leave the circus to attend classes

to become and EMT?" What the hell? Why did he care so much about this?

"Do you see my face? This is the face of someone who is freaking out. Put me down or I swear I will belt you with my broken arm...*which isn't broken*..."

Reece scowled, but he started walking again and she almost relaxed. At least she stopped gritting her teeth.

"I took a course over the summer when we were between seasons."

It figured that he'd focus on her dislike of the outside world, like that was important right now. She could do things outside the circus, she just didn't care to. When the circus off-seasoned at Bohannon Farm, as it did every year, it was like living at the circus. The only difference with the summer she'd gone to school had been that she'd had to spend time with a bunch of possibly dangerous weirdos who'd thought mowing the lawn every Saturday, frequenting the mall, and driving an SUV was something to brag about. "My trailer is that way." She pointed with her good arm, and he veered off, following the directions she supplied.

Within two minutes she was inside her cozy little home. "There's supplies in the skinny cabinet above the sink."

Reece put her down in front of the sink and the first thing he did was wash his hands. "Paper towels?"

She gestured to the other side of the counter and then opened the cabinet to start getting out supplies with her good arm, then thought better of it and stuck the bad one under the faucet. It would hurt, but if she was going to have pain she'd either control it or be the one in control of inflicting it.

Number-one rule or dealing with Reece? Don't let him hurt her again. Even if it was that for-her-own-good kind of hurt.

No, especially the for-her-own-good kind of hurt. She'd had enough of that, thank you very much.

"This doesn't look good," he muttered, as he wrapped his hand around her wrist to take control of the flow of water over the wound. In that second she forgot all about her fear for Gordy and about the pain. She even forgot about how angry she was at him for what he was about to do to them all. Skin-to-skin contact was more potent than being carried, especially when it reminded her of how big he'd gotten. Hadn't he supposed to have been full grown when he'd gone off to school? When did men stop getting bigger? Was he still growing? This was ridiculous.

Her chest ached when she looked up at him. "You're too tall. Makes my neck hurt." She pretended that was where the pain was. It was better than give in to the urge to press against him and lean into the strength she'd seen in action. Give in to the urge to keep forgetting the bad things. Soak in the comfort she knew waited in his arms.

Stupid.

That should be rule number two—don't let Reece comfort her ever again.

She pulled her arm from under the water and ripped a fresh paper towel from the roll to blot at it, then applied pressure to staunch the blood that started flowing again. The ache deep in her arm had subsided but it surged back to life when she put pressure on it. If she mentioned that, he'd have her at the emergency room faster than she could say, "Don't put me to sleep, it's just a broken arm." It'd be her front left leg if she were a quadruped, mirroring Gordy's injury. Fate's twisted sense of humor...

He caught her arm again and directed it under the counter light where he could examine the bite. It was well on its way to bruising and there were several ugly punctures and a shallow gash.

"It doesn't need stitches. There are a couple of punctures that I might put a stitch or two into, but if you have butterflies, that can hold for now." He watched her, his voice having lost that edge of irritation as soon as he'd gotten his way. His mouth hadn't got the news that he was less irritated, though. His lips pressed together, hard and cranky. "Probably better anyway, in case an infection does start up—which happens way more often in punctures than cuts, you realize. And the reason we should have gotten this treated faster."

He unfurled his fingers from her arm and her thinking cleared a little. She needed more of that. "You know, I can do the medicine and bandaging. You visit your mom. I need...I need you to go and I can take care of this myself." Him going would help. It had to help.

"I'm almost done." The way he no longer met her eyes said that he felt something at least. It might be a ghost of the connection that they'd once had, but he still felt something.

"I don't care if you're almost done. I want you to be somewhere else. Somewhere I'm not. I will finish up and then go back to the stables. You're messing everything up." Her voice rose as she spoke, reaching to near shrillness at the end. "Because...you're still..."

"You can be calm if you want to be calm." He sure sounded calm. But then she remembered—he didn't really care about them. This was just Doctor Man, who lived to treat patients. Or something.

"I'm trying to be calm. You could hurry up some. You know I need to get back." Gordy needed her. Focus on that. "Except I forgot that you're good at leaving people waiting." *No, don't focus on that. Gordy. Get it together.*

He gave her a look and snagged her wrist again—no doubt to keep her from getting away. She'd have to climb out the window in her bedroom or squeeze through the one over the sink if she wanted to get out. His big body blocked the tiny kitchenette. And he continued to work at his own pace.

She tried deep breaths to calm down. She really was trying, that was the problem. She'd thought she could always be calm, but right now she couldn't. Her heart hammered against her sternum like the beat of so many hooves in the ring. She could hear it, see it pulsing in her vision, and she knew that wasn't good. Her deep breaths got shallow and fast, outside her control.

Everything was out of control.

"They won't euthanize him while I'm gone, right?" she blurted out. "That's the kind of thing that takes time and preparation, right?" More words tumbled from her lips.

Like he knew anything. Or maybe he did. Maybe he was keeping her there forever for a reason. "They'd wait long enough to let people say goodbye if it came to that, right?"

Right? Right? God, she really did sound crazy. And she'd had a plan for speaking to him on the farm, when the dust had settled after they'd all settled in. Later. In the future.

"Take a deep breath. In through your nose," Reece said, his voice firm and demanding. He wanted to control everything. Even how she breathed!

"Jolie," he said her name again. "I think you're having a panic attack. Slow down your breathing."

"I'm not panic attacking." Was that even a term? She'd said it wrong. Everything was wrong. That's exactly the kind of inarticulate nonsense that would make him think twice about even considering her request when she got round to making it. And probably everything she'd said and done since she'd seen him again would add to that thinking twice and thrice, and whatever fourth, fifth and sixth were... Sure, no problem, he'd hand over the reins of his birthright to someone who might be a babbling idiot.

Jolie had no proof she could even lead picnic ants in a straight line to the potato salad. She knew she could do it. Or she thought she could. She'd been so sure before he'd got here. Before she'd fallen headlong into that deep place where she stuffed all the emotions that were too hard to put words to.

It would be better if she knew it in some logical manner that came with charts and graphs. Doctors probably loved charts and graphs!

"I can't breathe." She probably had caught some awful horse-bite disease. Everything was wrong. Everything.

He let go of her wrist suddenly and grabbed her hips. Half an accelerated heartbeat later she was sitting on the counter in front of him, gasping for air and shaking all over, helpless against the onslaught of tears that swamped her vision and poured down her cheeks.

Reece cupped her cheeks, tilting her head until he had her gaze. So blue. So steady.

He said something. His thumbs stroked her cheeks, wiping away the tears as they poured down. She had no idea what he was saying, calming sounds. Comforting sounds. And they reached her. The tears slowed along with her breathing, and behind them she felt a stampede of embarrassment. And confusion. What the heck had just happened...?

"That was a panic attack?" her voice rasped, the raw sound causing a few aftershock hiccups.

He nodded, wrapping his arms around her and pulling her to his chest. Warm. Firm. Right where she'd wanted to be.

"I've had some experience with them."

It was hard to imagine anything rattling Reece like this. "They're awful," she mumbled, drained, ashamed, and wantonly breaking rule number two.

"Yes, they are."

She'd stop breaking rule number two in a second, but right now she needed the hug. And with her face hidden by his chest she didn't have to look him in the eye...

When she didn't say anything else, he added, "They're your family, and they love Gordy too. They're not going to make any decisions while you're getting your injury tended to."

"I know. I'm sorry. I don't know why... I don't know what happened. I don't usually act like a crazy person." She swiped her eyes again and pulled away, before she did something even crazier.

It had just been the shock of seeing him again for the first time. But that shock was gone, it couldn't last forever. So it was done. She willed it to be done and she was the one in control of her emotions...not the other way around. Never again. Focus on one big emotion at a time, that was the key to remaining tethered to her sanity. And right now that one big emotion had to be concern for Gordy. He needed her. She could fall apart later.

Forget that the last time she'd been this scared she'd been sixteen and watching Reece drive away into the world alone, and remember how all the faith she'd put in him—all the worry she'd had for him—had meant nothing. In the end he had been just like her father, who, incidentally, had been good at hugging too.

She should remember all that. If Reece was going to consider her request, it wouldn't be because he cared so much about them. She had to find another angle. "You should finish." Because she'd freaked out before they'd got to bandaging.

He nodded, looked at her longer than she was comfortable with him looking, then resumed treatment—dabbing on ointment, placing a couple of rectangles of gauze onto the wound, which he had her hold in place so he could deal with the tape.

"Don't worry about this. You're just wound tight right now. We all are. I'm worried about him too." A couple of rips of tape later and he replaced her fingers with white cloth tape, guaranteed to hold even if she should bleed again and get the whole mess wet. "If it starts feeling hot or hurting more, tell me."

"I know. Antibiotics." She pretended he hadn't said anything about worrying about Gordy. He could turn his worry on and off like a light switch or he didn't really feel anything. Or Doctor Worry was different from the worry of mortal men who couldn't worry and fret over loved ones while ignoring them utterly.

"If I had my kit, I'd start you on them right now," he muttered, and smoothed down the last strip of tape. "You haven't got any bigger, have you?" He squinted at her in a way she could only deem as judgmental.

"I'm big enough. Not everyone aspires to be a giant's stunt double." Sarcasm: Her Refuge. Her voice-activated ten-foot pole for keeping things away, keeping things from getting to her.

"I'm not judging. I was considering your weight for prescription purposes."

"Oh." Okay, so maybe she wasn't totally done being crazy. But it was easier to jump to a negative conclusion than to think that he cared. He was still here to destroy her *everything*. Time to go. She slid off the counter on the other side of him and hurried to the door. "Lock it when you leave." Not waiting for an answer, she took the stairs at a near run.

"Do you want some pain relievers?" he called from behind her. She heard the question as the door swung shut but didn't go back inside to answer him. Pain relievers? Hell, yes, she'd like some. She'd also like some amnesia pills. And she'd like him to take them too and forget the last ten minutes.

Even if the small part of her mind that was currently sane said that no one would put Gordy down without giving her time to say goodbye, she was still more than half-terrified she'd get back to the stables and find him already gone.

Reece stared at the screen door for several seconds, expecting it to open again and for Jolie to come back for some ibuprofen or something. But she didn't.

He shook a couple of pills out, laid them on yet another paper towel and folded it around the pills so he could stick them in his pocket. Before the night was over, someone would need them. Possibly him. If he didn't know better, he'd say that panic attacks were contagious. That he'd somehow given her the one he'd been fighting all evening.

A mess of paper towels and tape littered the counter, so he spent time tidying it up before he left. That was one thing always ground into the circus kids: keep your living area tidy. When it's small, and on wheels, you had to be as tidy and deferential to everyone else as you could be. And you had to be okay with making things work, even if that meant taking a shower with the garden hose behind the RV because you were on a schedule and all the other showers were occupied. You learned to make the best of things. He could control the physical mess he left behind, and the only speculation he could offer to the emotional devastation he knew he'd leave in his wake? He could only hope that they could make the best of it.

It was their nature. It was *her* nature.

Three years age difference between them, but circus kids grew up fast. Especially Jolie. When they'd gotten her back, she'd never really been a normal little kid. Always looking over her shoulder. Always afraid something would go wrong. Children learned behavior, like worrying, and she'd learned it then and learned it well.

He'd spent the last ten years trying not to think about what she'd learned by him leaving.

He still didn't want to think about that, even with it staring him in the face.

His worry for Jolie could cripple him. It certainly would've had him running back home to her that first week away at school if he'd so much as let his mother mention her name. It had been his only survival tactic. The only way for him to stay in school had been to quit Jolie cold turkey.

She might be the same size, but she'd changed in other discouraging ways. He'd probably played a part in that. Thirty minutes in her presence had dredged up more questions than just how she was going to handle him closing down the circus.

The show music had stopped a while ago, so Mom was either at her RV or the mess tent. She always liked to eat with everyone. Keightly Circus really did band together as a family, which was the hardest part of shutting it down. They ate together. Off-seasoned together. Raised their children together. The elderly performers even tended to retire to the same places...

He flipped the lock on the doorknob and stepped out, giving it a good pull. Locked up. As requested. Now to find Mom and get more information.

An hour later, having received the lecture from his mother that Reece had been dodging for a decade, he walked into the stables with two plates and bottles of water.

He found Jolie alone with Gordy, who was now utterly unconscious. A simple cot had been slid into the remaining space in Gordy's stall and Jolie sat on it, her back to the wall and her legs dangling, eyes fixed on the small white stallion. Though by her glazed look, she wasn't really looking at Gordy.

Reece knew only too well that you could stare right into your past if left to your own thoughts long enough. Usually at the memories you least needed to focus on. The ones you'd probably be better off forgetting entirely.

Since he'd stepped foot onto the lot, when he'd had any time alone with his thoughts, he got images of his father's blood, muddying the sawdust and sand in the ring...

"What are you doing? You look sick. Is the food really that bad?" Jolie's voice cut through his haze. Thinking too hard was contagious too...

"It's fine. I'm fine. Brought dinner. Thought you might be hungry and I'd like to know what the vet said." He nodded toward the cot—it was big enough for both of them to sit on without touching each other, provided it stood the weight. "You mind?"

A suspicious squint answered him, but that was better than the panic earlier. Her green eyes still had that glassy look, like emotion wasn't too far beneath the surface. She was the first to look away, but she held up her good hand for the plate, freeing one of his so he could fish the water bottles from his pockets before he sat. "So?"

"He said front-leg breaks are worse than back, which aside from his circulation issues... I don't really under-stand." She rested the plate on her thigh, freeing her hands to shuffle the water bottle off to the other side. It must still be hurting. "Not sure if he means that they happen more frequently or if they are harder to splint, harder to heal, harder on the horse, or if it's Gordy-specific..." She gestured to the new harness on Gordy with the toe of her boot. "But that sling is more comfy and it's not bound by notches. They got it perfectly seated. Mack said it's pos-sible he twisted something inside when he fell, so it was good that we got him on his feet so fast. They couldn't feel anything when palpating his belly, but he was out of it by then and couldn't have told them it hurt even if the pain was blistering."

"Prognosis?" He looked at the food, not able to bring himself to take a bite yet. She hadn't either, even if she was using her feet to gesture so her hands could keep hold of her dinner. Well, hand. She wasn't using the injured arm for anything but keeping her water tucked against her thigh.

"Oh..." She breathed the word, her tone confirming the worst, and that she wouldn't agree with it until forced to. "He said it's rough... We would try..."

But.

She didn't actually say it but he still heard it.

He put his bottle down, fished the pills from his pocket and placed them beside her leg. "Anti-inflammatories," he murmured, leaving her to take them or not, and went back to the conversation about Gordy. "So what's the next step?"

"Sit with him. Keep him comfortable. Watch for signs of colic." She took the pills. "And I have both pain medicine and tranquilizers to inject if he gets worse."

"You did really well with the tranquilizer earlier. Hit the vein the first time. Did you take courses on animal care too?"

"No, I learned to care for people, but I've given injections and done blood draws on the horses before. And I read. A lot."

He remembered that. She read anything zoological in nature, didn't matter if it dealt with the horses and dogs that were in the show or wild animals, which had not been in the show since her twice great-grandfather had been mauled by a lion during an act. The circus was always dangerous, but it had got a little less dangerous when they'd got back to their roots and away from the exotic-animal fad popular from the Victorian era.

"Thank you for dinner."

He kept his eyes on the food, but not looking at her didn't keep memories at bay. He made himself eat. It would be a long night, as he had every intention of spending it here at her side. "You're welcome." He looked at her again. Dammit.

The wild auburn curls had been worked into some kind of fancy braid so he could see her clearly even in the dim light of the stable. Still the prettiest girl he'd ever seen in the flesh. Even prettier than when he'd left. She might have cried again since she'd left her trailer—her wide-set green eyes looked bigger, glassy, and heartbroken. There was a little crease between her brows that said she frowned more than she should, and even now, with her expression mostly blank, the shadow of that unhappy crease remained.

"I know it's not the right time for this, but I wanted to apologize," Reece said, feeling his way through the words as he went.

"For leaving us?"

CHAPTER THREE

No. He couldn't apologize for that. "For..." He looked at her again and drew a deep breath. "I mean about the circus. About what I'm here to do. I know it's not what you want, but I want to help you get settled wherever you want to go after Keightly."

"I don't want to go anywhere else," she said.

None of them did. He was the bad guy in this, but for the right reasons. One day she'd see that. "I know you don't."

She put the untouched plate aside and turned on the cot to face him. "Listen. I didn't expect to see you tonight. Actually, I didn't think I'd see you at all until Ginny and Mack's wedding. And what happened to Gordy...I had a plan for how it should go when you came to the farm. What I wanted to say... But it sort of evaporated when I freaked out."

She had a plan? She had pictured him coming back and it didn't involve being a crazy woman? "Don't say you wanted to talk me out of closing."

"I was going to ask you to work with me and change what we do. No more traveling circus, a new future."

That sounded an awful lot like "Please don't close".

"There is no future for Keightly, Jolie. This isn't just about me and what I want to do with my life. It's dangerous. Especially with people getting older, it's getting more dangerous for them. Gordy is an old-timer and—"

"He's not an old-timer," she cut in, the flash of her eyes telling him that the crazy woman might be about to make a reappearance if he didn't watch out. "He's twenty-eight. Miniature horses live much longer than big horses, and we have some big horses on the farm that are over thirty-five. Gordy is firmly middle-aged."

She was still afraid someone was going to announce plans to euthanize the little guy. "Not what I'm getting at."

"Number one, the big-spectacle acts, the ones that are the most dangerous, aren't done by the core troupe any more. We get contracts for the headliners—fliers. We had a Russian bar act a couple years ago. But just because the core group is getting older doesn't mean that they want to give up the life."

"I know they don't want—"

"Number *two*." She held up two fingers, silencing him. "I don't want to keep the circus on the road. I don't even want to keep it a circus."

"Not keep it a circus?" His headache was increasing. "Stop counting lists of supporting…whatever, and tell me what you want to do with Keightly."

"I want to make a circus camp," Jolie said, her voice softening. "At the farm."

"A circus camp."

"The older performers can still teach. I'm proof of that. Just because I don't perform any more doesn't mean I don't know how to do things. I can be the demonstration, they can instruct, and we can make sure to…to…" Her hands flew up, a gesture he knew was meant to summon some word that had temporarily eluded her, and which had always been his cue to finish her thought when her mouth got ahead of her. Not that he could do that any more.

"Circuses are dying." She abandoned that train of

thought and started again. "They're dying out. There were probably thousands in North America, now how many are left? How many close every year? How long before these art forms are no longer even remembered? Sooner, if we don't teach them to children and pass on our knowledge. Plus, we're only half an hour from Atlanta, and people love Keightly in this part of Georgia. They'd love to send their children to circus camp in the summer. Physical activity, fun, a day camp while their parents work. And for the rest of the year we could do the circus-school thing for older kids. Like high school and college age, those who are at their most fit and can best handle the rigors."

"Wait." He lifted a hand to rub his forehead, a headache blazing to life dead center behind his eyes. It wasn't exactly asking him to keep things going as they were, and while he appreciated that... "You make good points. All your points are good, but Mom is done with running things. She's said so over and over again and that's why I'm here. But I don't have time to devote to co-running a circus camp. I have a practice to build and run."

"I'm not asking Ginny or you to run anything. I'm offering. I will run it. I can do it. I'm not a little girl any more." It wasn't that she didn't like being told no, she just wouldn't be told no about *this*. Her fingers twitched then drummed against her legs, trying to calm her indignation. "You do whatever it is you want, focus on your practice. Ginny can retire and participate however much or little she wants to."

"My name is on it, this is my equipment, I'll have to take a hand in it. Plus, there's also no way I want to subject children to that kind of danger."

"I wouldn't just welcome them and throw them on the trapeze without a net," Jolie said, and then winced, realizing how badly chosen her words had been for him. "We'd be safe. Start slow. Probably start with simple tumbling for children without any gymnastic experience. And it's not all acrobatics. You know as well as anyone that there are a blue million different disciplines within the circus that don't even approach performance. Including costume design, set designs, tending animals..."

"People like you who don't perform any more."

"Right." She stopped looking him in the eye, shifting her gaze back to the sleeping Gordy.

Because she'd basically told him to stuff it earlier when he'd asked why she hadn't been dressed to perform. He couldn't tell if she didn't want to talk about that or if she just didn't want to talk about it with him. Screw it, he wanted to know! If it was another of his sins, he had to know so he could fix it. "When did you stop?"

"I stopped when you did."

His stomach lurched. "Why?"

She shrugged. "I just did."

"You had to have had a reason. You loved it..."

She shrugged again. "I didn't want to any more."

"Jolie—"

"I still practice, do different things, it's a good way to keep in shape. I don't do the trick-riding, but I figure the rest of the Bohannons have that market cornered anyway."

She didn't cast blame on him, and that was something he should be thankful for. What could he say if she brought up his past sins? And why was he digging into her history and motivations when he really didn't want her digging into his? Because he was an idiot. Because he couldn't know her without wanting to know every single thing about her.

Because he couldn't say no to her, which was why he had stayed as far away as he'd been able to.

And it was because he couldn't say no to her that he had to get out of there now. Bad plan to stay with her. "Are you going to be all right here on your own tonight?"

"Yes. Someone will come and try to relieve me in a few hours." She looked him fully in the eye again, somehow managing to look even smaller on the cot beside the unconscious horse. "Will you at least think about it?"

He knew what he thought about it. He thought—no, he knew—it was a bad idea. No matter how badly she wanted it.

"Please? Give me some time to show you how it can be. After Gordy is stable enough that he doesn't need me round the clock? After we relocate to the farm?"

After her arm healed? After he told her he had a probable buyer for all the equipment?

He stretched to buy a few seconds in the vain hope the right words would appear, present him some way to let her down easily, but his words were as elusive as hers had been. "Okay. I'll wait until we've settled at the farm, see what everyone else thinks about the idea. Weigh the pros and cons…"

She breathed out slowly, in what he could only term as relief, and leaned back against the wall. "Don't take this the wrong way, but could you also stay away from me for a few days?"

"Why?"

She shrugged. "Because if you're around, I'll just keep wanting to ask you to do it, and then—" She stopped suddenly, her cheeks flaring pink. "Well, not *do it*, obviously, because that would be stupid. Obviously." She was repeating herself so she stopped, shook her head, and then tried again. "I wasn't talking about sex. Obviously."

If she said "obviously' again…

"We don't…not sex. I wasn't talking about doing that. Hah." She shook her head. The more she tap-danced around, trying to clarify, the worse it got. "I meant doing… the camp. I would keep asking you to do the camp…" A great sigh came from her and she stopped talking. Finally. Without more obviouslys.

"Sure," he said, working to keep his voice normal. Unaffected. "I can give you space. You should sleep. Mom's got my number if you think the bite's growing infected. I need to go take care of some things anyway." He walked out.

He had important things to do, like locating his backbone before he just said yes to whatever she wanted to keep from letting her—and everyone else—down.

It was like that. The reason he didn't want them in the circus any more? He didn't want any one hurt. Any kind of hurt. But physical hurt—which could kill—had to trump emotional hurt. The emotional hurt just made you feel like you were dying.

They would acclimate to life off the road and outside the circus, he reminded himself yet again. And if they couldn't, he'd help them find new homes. Somewhere he could stop worrying about them. Somewhere someone else would have to take responsibility when luck turned and those death-defying feats could no longer defy.

Since the second his father had died, that responsibility had passed to him, and even when he hadn't actively been with the circus, he'd felt it. Oh, he'd ignored the hell out of it, but now that he could no longer do that he felt the weight of every life in his hands. And it was about damned time he used those hands to shield them.

He was a man now, not a boy to be shushed and ignored.

And really not a horny teenager who kept replaying Jolie's clumsy words: *I'll just keep asking you to do it.*

There had been moments in Jolie's life when the instant she'd done something, she'd regretted it.

Usually, those moments had involved falling off something. When she'd first started learning the wire, she'd had that feeling a lot. It had always gone away as soon as she'd hit the ground.

Since she'd learned to control her emotions, she'd not experienced this level of regret over anything she'd done.

And that feeling had never lasted for three days before.

She couldn't stop worrying about her sudden anxiety-driven freak-out and the way it painted her. More evidence that she was losing her mind. Her practiced, easy, unflappable calm had abandoned her the second she'd seen him, and even though he'd stayed away, as she'd asked, she couldn't shake it.

The very last show had run last night. Jolie had not attended. The show had ended for her the night Gordy had been hurt.

Today she should be doing what she always did—helping load everything with the others—but Mack had come and told her to stick with her charge. Maybe he heard about the freak-out. Maybe it was in deference to her arm. She had no idea.

So she did what she could in the stables, tried to wipe her mind, and tried to ignore the ache in her arm and the worry over how Gordy would fare during the ride to the farm. There could be no sling in the back of the trailer, not with it bumping down the highway and over potholed country roads. He'd have to lie down.

People came and went, carrying out equipment and moving out the other horses.

Jolie disassembled the cot and set it out, then resumed her vigil from a small stool in the stall. That was something she could do. Now, if only she could stop feeling like she'd just made the biggest misstep in history and at any second she was going to fall. No, actually, it was more like at any second she was going to stop falling. A sudden bone-crunching, sixty-to-zero-in-the-blink-of-an-eye method of stopping.

It might just be a relief when it finally happened. The fall was just killing her more slowly.

If she hadn't turned into a crazy person, Reece could've come today and waved his big stupid arms and impressive shoulders around to move Gordy when he needed it. Or lift him up in the horse trailer if his belly started bothering him when they were on the road. The poor little horse was still under the effect of drugs, and she couldn't tell whether his innards were out of sorts or if he was just too out of it to eat enough for any sort of digestive motility. Any time he flicked his ear, she checked for poo, and celebrated even a little bit of the stuff.

She looked behind Gordy again.

"You need help with him in the trailer?" a deep male voice asked, and this time she recognized it instantly.

Great. He would show up while she had her head right down there by the horse's butt.

"I'm not doing anything!" Jolie blurted out, jerking her head back from Gordy's rear quarters, "Just looking for horse poo." Right, because she wanted to remind him that she was inarticulate. She should've said a clinical word. Who in the world over the age of ten said "poo'?

"I didn't ask what you were doing," Reece said, grinning at her for the first time in over a decade.

"Sorry. I'm really tired." And she'd blame that on her acting like a crazy person this time. "What did you say?"

"I asked if you need help with Gordy."

"I do. Yes. Please." Jolie took a deep breath and peeled herself up off the stool. "I'm stressing about getting him home. And about—"

"Whether he's developing colic," Reece filled in, understanding her fecal fixation, thank God. "Have you changed the bandage?"

"Not since yesterday…I think." Maybe. The past three days were a bit of a blur.

He lifted a leather case and gave it a rattle. "Lucky for you I came prepared this time."

"Lucky for me." She glanced at Gordy again and then stepped toward Reece. "Maybe we could do this outside. I think I need a little air before we get crammed into a horse trailer. Wait, that's what you meant, right? Riding with me and Gordy in the trailer?"

"That is what I meant," he confirmed, stepping to the side to let her pass and then following her out into the sunny spring morning.

They always loaded the animals and outbuildings first, mostly because they were done taking them down first. The Bohannons would likely be on the farm before the workers were even done pulling down and packing up the big top that had put food in their bellies for years.

She tried to put that out of her mind. It wasn't the last time she'd see the tent. It'd go up again for his mother's wedding, whatever Reece decided about the camp. She sat at a picnic table and laid her arm on the sun-warmed wood, then let her eyes wander away from whatever he was going to do.

She added a new rule to her growing list intended to help her learn to traverse this new, overly emotional landscape.

Rule number three—focus on one emotion at a time.

Picking one emotion right now was harder than when her terror for Gordy had had her by the throat. Reece's presence made it hard to think. Not having slept much for the past three days also made it hard to think, and she'd already gone two for two with crazy Jolie appearing whenever Reece did.

Made her not want to ask if he'd come to any decision. To talk about something less like emotional napalm.

"Do you remember when I used to ride Gordy?" She felt him flicking at the tape and within a few seconds the bite was exposed, and the open feel made her look.

"I remember." His voice changed, a softening that gave her some small hope that he had something in his heart for their history, their lineage...other than just the horror and tragedy of his father's death.

"It wasn't long before I was too big for him. For a long time I asked when he'd grow up so I could ride him again. I didn't understand he was different from the other horses," she murmured, feeling the familiar burn return to her eyes. Three days of it springing up. Three days of waiting to fall. Three days of insanity. "He can be such a brat sometimes. He bites the other horses all the time. But this was the first time he ever bit me."

Reece almost reached for her hand but pulled back at the last second in favor of the medical supplies. "He didn't mean to."

Jolie swallowed, shifting her gaze away from him again. It took her a while to work up the will to speak and the ability to trust her voice. "I know."

"It's looking good." He shifted them away from the sad topic and back to something he could control. "The punctures at least. Better than I hoped, but there's more bruising than I like. You should get it X-rayed, just to be on the safe side." Reece uncapped a fresh bottle of water and poured some over gauze pads to clean the wound.

"If it's broken it's just a tiny fracture. That might not show up on the films for a couple of weeks. I'll wait a little bit and see how it goes." She continued shifting the topic. "Have you been staying with your mom?"

"No. I have a short-term apartment leased. I haven't been here at all since that first night, though I meant to come back. One of my professors called to advise me about a doctor in the area who is retiring and wants to transition his practice into the hands of another. He set us up to speak and it's actually pretty close to the farm."

"Who's the doctor?"

"Richards."

"Oh, I know him. He's got great peaches, and planted more at his orchard not long ago. Doing something with apples. I kind of zoned out when he was explaining that part." She shook her head. "Something about apple breeding, which sounded weird and not like something I wanted to know. It might forever ruin me on apples."

Reece applied antibiotic ointment then started tearing strips of tape to get ready for bandaging. But he stopped when she mentioned knowing Dr. Richards. "Have you seen him?"

"Granny Bohannon sees him, and I've taken her to the doctor several times. Practically have to hogtie her to get her there, no matter how bad she's feeling," she answered, and when he didn't immediately respond, she prompted, "I haven't seen him for my own health, if that's somehow weighing in on your decision on whether to get in on his practice or whatever. You wouldn't get me grandfathered in as a patient."

"I'm not worried about that," he said, getting the bandage supplies together and finally moving on to the application stage.

Jolie squinted a little. Lying. He was lying. "You *are* worried about that."

"I'm more worried about other things."

"Are you sick?" Jolie looked him in the eye again. "Or are you worried that I'm going to freak out again?"

"Neither."

"You're lying." She resisted the urge to turn his head so he faced her. "You've looked like you're about to puke at least three times since you came back. So either you're sick or I make you sick."

"You don't..." Reece smoothed the tape down with his fingertips and Jolie finally noticed it wasn't just the hand-pat he aborted to avoid touching her, he was working hard not to touch her even while treating her arm. "It's the sawdust."

Sawdust? "Have you developed an allergy?"

"No. I just don't like the sawdust. Haven't been able to stomach the smell since Dad died." His voice was low and sincere, but gruff like he really didn't like admitting this. "The college I attended? The main old academic building where pretty much all the core classes were was remodeled during my first year. I learned to come in through the back door and take the long way to my classes to avoid it."

Jolie felt her stomach bottom out. All the time she'd spent with him after his father's death and she hadn't picked up on that? He hadn't even looked at her when he'd made this admission, which told her that it was something he felt vulnerable about. Reece still had some of his tells, though she obviously didn't know them as well as she'd always thought she did if this news was such a shock to her.

She'd never met anyone who didn't like the smell of sawdust before. That Keightly Circus used it to the end was a point of pride to them and the deep-rooted circus traditions they'd always tried to preserve while other outfits had grown bigger and more modern.

"So you wouldn't throw up?"

"No. That would have been okay. It was the panic I couldn't handle. Got over the worst of it, no real panic any more. Still makes me queasy, though."

"I'm sorry." She didn't know what else to say, but she did know that he needed some kind of contact—and she just didn't think her over-emotional self could handle him pulling away if she tried to touch him. At least it didn't seem like he was just being difficult any more. "I didn't know."

"I didn't want anyone to know. I still don't," he admitted in a low voice. "Just wanted you to know it wasn't you. But I think you were right about trying to keep some distance right now. It would be easy for things to get confused between us. Taking it slow would be for the best."

"I agree." She pulled her freshly bandaged arm away, stood, and began gathering the refuse. "They've already left with the other horses. We have a trailer to ourselves. We can get him in there and get on the road now if you're ready."

He nodded, gathered his supplies and approached the truck, where he handed his treatment bag to the driver and asked on his way back to her, "Is he tranquilized?"

"I hate that word. Makes it sound like such a peaceful state, and most everyone or everything I've ever seen tranquilized ended up slack-jawed and drooling." Jolie headed into the stables, Reece behind her. "But to answer your question, yes."

She peeked to make sure he was still out of it, that the poo fairy hadn't shown up while she was outside, and then unhooked the sling as Reece worked his magic muscles and lifted the horse to carry him to the trailer.

"You need to prepare yourself. If he's not doing any better after three days…" Reece began, leading where he knew Jolie didn't want to go. They were sitting in the hay in the trailer, Gordy between them, his head in her lap.

"Don't," Jolie whispered, emotion in her voice pulling at his insides.

"I'm not trying to hurt you."

"No, I know you think you're being practical, delivering the hard doctorly advice and whatever, but I'm not giving up on him while there's hope."

Denial. "Is there hope?"

She'd probably held out hope for him for months. He

hoped not, but he didn't know. And he didn't really want to know yet. Her emotional state wasn't the only reason Reece wanted to go slow with her.

"Of course there's hope. He's still alive." She looked at him like he was a monster, but she already had too many weapons to use against him to admit how gutted he would be when Gordy died. Admit how easily she could gut him if she wanted to. She probably didn't know she had any weapons at all, and his only chance was if she continued not to realize it.

"When we get to the farm and we get him situated in his sling, you need to wean him off all the drugs and see how he feels when he's alert."

"He's in pain."

"Yes, he is." Reece gave in to his decision not to touch her and laid his hand over her forearm, where the thin material of her sleeve would keep flesh-to-flesh contact at bay.

It was enough. She looked at him. "He stuck by me when I was in pain." Even with the sleeve barrier, she pulled her arm away. "It was just you, me and Gordy. When I got back. When Mom got me back from that awful group home when Dad left me. Just you and me, and Gordy. And he never left." She looked back at him and resumed petting the sleeping horse. "Dad left. You left. Gordy never left. I won't leave him to the whims of Fate. We're going to fight, and he'll get better."

He didn't know whether she was talking about just Gordy any more, or if she'd included herself in that declaration.

All he knew for sure was that he didn't like being lumped into the same category as her gutless father.

CHAPTER FOUR

REECE DIDN'T LIKE to sort through emotions. He ignored them as best he could until it all became clear without reflection. But nothing regarding Jolie was clear.

Well, nothing except the fact that she could still drive him crazy in every meaning of the word—even when he'd not seen or heard from her for two weeks.

Reece pulled into the long country driveway and reached up to loosen his tie, which seemed to be growing tighter and tighter the closer he got to the farm. The old quote about the road to hell being paved with good intentions rolled around in his head.

The old proverb was embroidered on a pillow in Dr. Richards's office, the practice he'd finalized purchase of in the past two weeks. If Richards didn't take that damned pillow with him when he left, Reece was going to burn it.

The road to hell wasn't paved with anything, let alone intentions. It was a long gravel driveway into the middle of nowhere Georgia.

His mother's wedding would start in about an hour, so here he was, no solution and no idea what he was walking into, or how the temperament of the group would be. All he knew was he'd grown really tired of waiting for a solution to the camp question. Jolie was probably tired of waiting too. If she wanted to open in time for summer, there was definitely a clock on his decision-making process.

The white summer big top had been raised, and Reece pulled up far enough to the side that he wouldn't be disturbing any post-wedding photo ops, and got out. Spring was always a volatile time in the South, and with the weather growing ever hotter, a cold front from the northwest promised something nasty. In the distance he could see black clouds looming, and already the wind had picked up.

He rolled up the windows of his car, grabbed his jacket and wandered into the tent.

No one was inside yet, but flowers and an arch of some sort stood in the ring.

Reece took the opportunity to check for sawdust, and breathed in deeply, braced for the revulsion he expected to follow.

"It's just sand." Jolie's soft voice came from off to the side, refocusing his attention on her.

She sat on the end of the bleacher, her pale auburn curls pinned up on the side by a flower, lots of milky skin on display, a lightly freckled shoulder bared by the filmy pink dress she wore.

No solution there either. The only thing he could think of was: girl next door. "Thank you." It was kind of her to see to that, though she might want to hurt him.

Jolie looked him over, noting the extremely well-cut suit. "You had that tailored? It looks tailored. Your mom will be pleased."

"Does that mean I look good?" Reece wandered over and leaned an elbow on the edge of the bleacher, right by where she sat. His elbow almost touched her thigh, so she slid down the seat a little.

"You look good. If they don't move up the time, though, I imagine no one will look good for it."

"Storm?"

"Storm." She tilted her head toward the entrance he'd come through and added, "I stashed a bucket of gloves, hammers and ropes back there, just in case the wind starts wreaking havoc with the tent." Because even if Reece wasn't going to let her use it, she couldn't just let it fly away in a strong wind.

"Good idea."

"I wasn't sure you'd be here," she murmured, looking back at the ring and decidedly away from him.

"At my mom's wedding?"

"It's been two weeks." She'd made up her mind not to bring up any of the camp business with him today if he came, so she probably shouldn't pick a fight with him because he'd been gone without word again for two weeks. And really it was dumb to be upset about it, and she wouldn't be upset about it if he didn't leave her hanging in limbo again. This time it wasn't about their personal relationship, it was about their possible professional relationship. Which probably meant that it shouldn't actually upset her.

Besides, Reece didn't need her giving him an excuse to abandon everyone again. They were all happy he'd come back, the prodigal son. If she ran him off, they'd forgive her—that's what family did—but it would hurt them and most of Jolie's existence was focused on protecting these people, not unthinkingly hurting them.

So maybe she should take a page out of Reece's book and avoid him.

She stood up, smoothed down the one-shoulder pale pink chiffon dress she'd gotten especially for this wedding, and walked away from him to the stairs so she could walk down. His eyes followed her to the end, and once on the ground she turned in the other direction and walked away from him.

"Do you have something you need to do?" he called

after her, sounding confused. Welcome to her world. He left her in a perpetual state of confusion.

Did she have something she needed to do? Not really.

"Yes," she lied, sort of, not looking back at him. Did it count if that thing she needed to do was find somewhere to continue their decade-long tradition of not talking to one another?

She felt him following and stopped to look back. "What are you doing?"

"Helping?" Reece shrugged, like this was perfectly normal.

"The thing I need to do is be alone. It's your mother's wedding, and having us at each other's throats or acting crazy would be bad."

"So let's not act crazy," Reece said, shrugging again. "Truce for a day?"

"Stop shrugging. It just draws attention to your gigantic shoulders," Jolie grumbled. "Truce? Easier said than done."

He reached up and pushed back a stray lock of sandy brown hair, tucking it behind his ear. The rest of his mane stayed caught in a short ponytail at the base of his skull, but that one lock kept breaking free, making her itch to touch it.

"Do you hate me, Jo?"

What?

Right. He wasn't talking about his hair.

"Sometimes," Jolie murmured, refusing to lie about that, even if it wasn't an admission she wanted to make. "I also don't want to bother you, and I don't want to fight with you...which is kind of a lie because I do want to fight with you. Or actually, I want to yell at you. And maybe kick you in the junk. But that would be bad. Counterproductive. Pathetic. And it's exhausting."

She stopped her random confession because dealing

with any sort of feelings meant she might get uncontrol-
lably teary. Something else she'd discovered in the past
two weeks. People weren't supposed to cry *before* the wedding. She should save up her tears for the wake to follow.

He reached up and tugged on his tie, loosening it
around his neck.

"You're messing it up."

"You said that before. I'm messing everything up. I
know. And I don't care. I can't breathe." Reece worked at
his collar until the tie was hanging loose and the top but-
ton was unfastened.

Jolie closed her eyes and took a deep breath, seeking
strength from somewhere.

He stepped over to her, stopping close enough that even
with her eyes closed she knew she'd have to crane her neck
to look him in the eye. Nothing touched, but she felt heat
radiating off him. "I know you said you want to kick me
in the junk, but aside from this unexpected violent streak
you've developed you look amazing."

"I don't...it's the dress. It's new." She opened her eyes,
forcing herself to meet his eyes.

"I thought it was bad manners for anyone to outshine
the bride."

"And you haven't even seen the bride yet."

"I know a tough act to follow when I see one." Reece
ran the tip of his finger over the pink orchid pinned in her
hair and his voice quieted. "I didn't know I wasn't going
to come back when I first left."

Every survival instinct in her roared to life, demanding
she step back, put some space between them, not look at
him...but closed eyes didn't hold tears well, and the fool
seemed bound and determined to make her cry. "Please,
don't do this now."

"Can we just pretend for today that I haven't been an
ass for the past ten years?" A ghost of a smile danced

across his lips. "That I'm just the owner's idiot son? Bossy, opinionated, incapable of keeping his hands out of your hair... And you the big-hearted girl-next-door who puts up with me?"

"I never just put up with you," Jolie whispered, looking down and drawing a deep breath. They were having a moment. That needed to stop. She stepped back and put on her best sarcastic tone. "I suffered you."

"Did you?" Reece grinned despite her sour words.

Jolie mustered a smile and nodded. "Totally. Important distinction." And then she drew a breath. "Okay. I'll sit with you. For a little while."

"Just until you feel moved to violence against Samson again?" He turned, offering her his elbow.

Jolie laughed, unable to help herself. "You've named your manly bits? Good Lord, what an ego." But she slipped her hand through the crook of his arm. "Why would you name him after a mobile phone?"

"Samson is the strong dude from the Bible. Not the people who make electronics."

"Duly noted." Jolie tried to resist the urge to remind him how strong Samson *hadn't* been the only time she'd gotten up close and personal with him. And wait a minute, did that make her Delilah? Okay. Weird.

"Well if I start feeling violent toward him, I'll stay until I've carried out whatever instinct is telling me to do."

The wind picked up, buffeting the tent so hard that the thick vinyl thumped like a drum in the cavernous tent interior and saved her from reflecting too hard on the sudden bizarre ramifications of their genitals.

"If they don't hurry, they might end up getting married in Oz." Her hand tingled where it was wrapped around his arm, and even with the not inconsiderable heels she wore, he still towered over her. A feeling crept in with his presence and proximity that she refused to name. It was a stupid feeling, the kind of feeling that led her to all sorts of bad decisions.

They climbed a few rows up and sat, Jolie making sure she left some space between them, and while they waited for everyone else to get there, he talked. Safe topics.

It began with a story about his first day in residency, and how his size had auto-selected him to wrestle some naked, violent drunk down while others had got restraints on the man, and how he'd never been so happy to see insane amounts of body hair. "It was almost like he had on a fur suit, so that's what I pretended. Actually, I was a little envious at his ability to grow hair."

"You're really stuck on that Samson story, aren't you?" Jolie teased, but by the end of the story he had her laughing and, at least for the moment, distracted from all the crap that had piled up between them.

When the bride and groom entered the big top on foot, Jolie sat up straighter. "I thought they were going to ride in."

"Horseback?"

"That had been the plan." She shrugged. "Maybe they decided—" A crack of thunder stopped her words. Everyone looked up, including Reece.

As if Mother Nature had generously waited for the happy couple to find shelter first, as soon as they made their way to the ring, the sky opened up and rain poured down in such heavy amounts it echoed loudly in the nearly empty tent.

Lightning and thunder arrived, and the winds picked up, rocking the whole thing. Big storms made circus people nervous, but in the spirit of enjoying the wedding, everyone got out of their seats and moved to the outer edge of the ring so they could hear the vows.

Before the pastor had got out the "Dearly Beloved," a

whistle cracked through the air and in that instant forty heads turned in unison toward the direction the storm was rolling in from.

One of the anchor cables had come loose.

"Damn." Jolie took off in the direction where she'd stashed supplies and grabbed gloves, a couple of extra spikes and a hammer. A group ran with her, cousins and circus cousins along with Reece, all dragging on gloves and making ready to do whatever was needed to save the tent.

When another cable snapped free, the rest of the wedding party descended on the northwest side of the tent to hold it down.

Like hang-gliding in a hurricane, they worked between gusts to pound the stakes deeper into the earth. While a group worked on what had come free, others split off with hammers to drive in deeper the spikes that were still set, trying to ensure that they did not come free.

By the time they had the tent secure, every member of the wedding party was drenched and exhausted. All except the bride and groom, who were only severely disheveled, having been kept inside the tent working under threat of death or bodily harm.

Once again everyone gathered around the ring, the windblown bride and groom with the pastor the only three dry people under the big top.

Jolie stepped between Reece and Natalie, another cousin. As it became clear that the meager number of attendees couldn't fill the circumference of the center ring, they stepped inside and the circle of people closed ranks.

There was no bride's side or groom's side, they simply clasped hands and witnessed the joining of two lives.

For the first time in ten years Reece's hand opened beside her and she slipped her hand into his—palms crossed, fingers curling around the edges. Not entwined, not as lovers holding hands. As family. Just as Natalie's hand did on her left, minus that exaggerated tingle Reece always evoked.

But she had to ignore that.

Jolie would never have thought herself one to cry at weddings, and she didn't want to be one of those overly emotional people who did. It was just her stupid inner sixteen-year-old who'd dreamed of a Keightly-Bohannon wedding all those years ago.

That would have been different, of course. She could still remember what her ridiculous sixteen-year-old-self had imagined. Naturally, they would have gotten married on the trapeze, with flowers and vines wound around everything, culminating with her leaping into his arms with some ridiculously intricate trick that no one had ever tried before, spontaneously erupting from her in a flash of romantic inspiration... And then Reece would have caught her and kissed her and tossed her back.

Or the other one, where Gordy was the flower girl.

Every fantasy beyond ridiculous. Not at all romantic. Not like this ceremony, no matter what calamity conspired to interrupt it. In the end it simply stripped away any artifice and left the simple beauty and truth of two people who'd waited for each other...and had finally found their way together.

Her throat thickened. Maybe Reece had been right to leave when he had. Maybe she'd spun some fantasy about their relationship too. Maybe he'd known where she hadn't.

And now they were all so wet that maybe no one would notice a couple of tears on her cheeks...

Reece's hand squeezed, letting her know he'd noticed.

She looked up at him, but he did not look back at her. The way his jaw bunched confirmed for her that he wasn't unaffected now. The strange beast stood there, grinding his teeth. She couldn't even tell if he was reacting to his mother marrying or if she was the only one lost in those old thoughts.

And her doubts grew as the ceremony progressed. At the end hands eventually parted to applaud the new Mr. and Mrs. Mack Bohannon, leaving Reece as the last in the Keightly line. Maybe he was thinking about his dad.

Of course he was thinking about his dad...

"Are you all right?" she asked him as Natalie retrieved her camera and began snapping pictures of the newlyweds.

"They're taking pictures," Reece said, shaking his head.

Jolie nodded slowly. "It's a wedding. I think picture-taking has been the tradition as long as there have been photos."

"Yes, but look at everyone."

She looked at herself, at him, and at everyone else. She saw lots of clothing plastered against bodies, lots of wind-blown hair, and lots of smiles.

But it was definitely out of control.

"You think that the wedding was ruined by the storm." She reached up and turned his head until he was looking at his mom. "Do they look unhappy?"

"No." He wrapped his hand around her wrist and pulled her hand from his cheek. Without warning, he walked to the seats, grabbed his jacket and walked back. A second later he'd wrapped it around her and now busily buttoned it up, like that would keep the exceedingly oversized thing on her. "They look happy," he said when her arms were in the sleeves and he'd gotten her as warm as he could. "But it should have been better."

"It was pretty amazing the way it was."

"The tent almost blew away. We're all soaked. Her flowers are all broken."

"And her heart is full." She shook her head. He couldn't

focus on anything but the parts that were outside his control. "How about me? Do I look happy? Or am I just putting up a good front?" She smiled, though it was a guarded thing. She wasn't going to make this easy on him.

Reece looked at her over the space of several increasing heartbeats. "You were crying earlier."

He caught her arm again and his hands, big and much warmer than hers, closed around hers to warm it.

"I'm okay. A little cold, though, so thank you for the jacket."

"I know you're cold." He chuckled then said, "I'm pretty sure everyone knows that. It was a public service that I put that jacket on you."

"Public service?"

He looked at her now hidden chest, a glimmer of that old flirty light in his eyes.

"I'm sure your cold perkiness was making your male cousins uncomfortable."

Nipples. He was thinking about breasts, even though she didn't have a lot going on in that department. And that wasn't unappreciated. Except for the old rule that predated Reece, and which she should make rule number four, so she didn't forget that it applied to Reece as much as to other men.

She didn't need a man in her life. Better to be alone than with someone who would leave you anyway when he left the circus and the life. A variation on the rule ground into her head by her mother: don't marry a man not part of the circus—he'll only break your heart and abduct your daughter when he leaves.

Only there was no circus now, and she hadn't really revisited that rule.

She glanced over her shoulder to make sure no one was looking at them.

When she looked back, his hand was at the side of her

head, fiddling with the hair clip. He untangled it from the bits the wind had yanked free of the clip before dumping gallons of water on her and unwound the coil of curls. "The mess really is bothering you."

"I like it down."

"Even when it's all wet?"

"Especially when it's all wet..."

Her scalp tingled and the hooded quality of his eyes when he looked at her made everything else tingle too.

Damn rule number four. Their truce was in effect until tomorrow, and why couldn't that truce include all the other bad feelings she wanted a night off from?

Flirting, holding hands, kissing...all good feelings. Feelings she might like to try out again.

Giving in to impulse, Jolie stepped between his legs, where he perched on the side of the ring, and leaned up to press her lips to his stubbled cheek.

"What are you doing?" It didn't come out as a question so much as a gruff and somewhat alarmed statement, but his arms went around her nevertheless.

"Pretending you haven't been an ass for ten years." She slid her arms beneath his and turned her head to rest her cheek in the hollow of his shoulder.

His chin came down to rest atop her head, but his body didn't relax.

"You're warm."

"No, I'm not."

Jolie ran her hands up his spine, over the wet material, which thankfully was thin enough to have started drying. With a slow, drawn-out sigh Reece relaxed against her.

"I think they're doing the cake thing," he murmured into her hair, and Jolie turned her head to look, unwilling to pull back yet.

"I think they're in a hurry to get on to the wake and then on to their honeymoon."

"The wake?"

Jolie leaned back and looked at him, her brows pinched. "Yes..."

"For?"

"Keightly Circus? Did you really think we wouldn't have a wake for it?"

"But this is a wedding."

"And your mom and Mack wanted to celebrate a new beginning while we toasted the past. This is how they met, you know. It's balancing something sad with something good."

"They're moving the flower— What are they doing?" Reece's scowl forced her to pull back so she could see and explain to him properly what was going on.

"They're changing the set for the show."

"Performing..."

"I know you've been gone a while, but think. What do we usually do at a wake?" She wrapped his arms around her middle and stepped back until her back fully pressed into his chest.

What do they do at wakes? "Talk...about people. Drink some toasts..."

"And we give tributes." She shook his arm.

"It's been a long time since you checked on Gordy." He did not want to attend the wake. Not telling him was a dirty trick. Dirty. And if it weren't his mother's wedding day, he'd leave and let her riddle out the enigma of how he felt about this.

"No. Gordy's much better, which you would know if you hadn't stayed away entirely for two weeks." She turned in his arms and laid her hands on his chest. This felt good. Jolie felt right. A wake did not.

"Are you okay? No one's mad at you, if that's what you're worried about."

"I'm fine." The look she gave him said she knew better.

"You're nervous. Your hand is sweaty."

"It's fine. Let's sit." Reece let go and started walking, but Jolie caught his hand before he got too far. Surprise caused him to stop and look at her.

She squeezed his hand. "Don't look so grim."

There had better be actual drinks involved in these toasts. Something to let him turn this off. He let her go ahead of him up the bleachers, and followed.

In the first row someone had set out a line of framed photos. It only took a glance to establish who they were—people Keightly had lost over the years. Some he remembered, some only the older members of the group remembered.

Grandpa. Uncle. Cousin... The wakes he'd attended.

Dad. The wake he'd skipped.

This wake was sounding worse and worse all the time. Mechanically, he sat beside her.

"You'll wish you'd stayed," she whispered, accurately reading his mind. But she still kept her voice low, keeping his discomfort private, like she'd apparently kept the sawdust business private.

"The executioner doesn't usually attend the funeral."

"No one thinks of you that way. They love you, Reece."

She took his hand again, and he ignored the warning in his head that told him he shouldn't be touching her so much. Her hand felt good. Small, but strong. That touch. If this evening was going to go the way he thought it would, he'd need that touch to get him through.

"And as weird as you may feel right now, it's your family too. Everyone wants you here. Well, maybe not everyone—you don't seem to want you here. But everyone else does."

"Even you?"

Jolie nodded, but the sadness never far from her eyes filled in what that nod didn't. She didn't want to want him there. She'd told him to stay away, after all, and he had no doubt that however bothered by everything he was, she was just as affected. He just didn't know whether that was a good thing or a bad thing. All he knew was that it was impossible to ignore.

The lights went down and she scooted a little closer to him. He switched her hand to his other and wrapped the closest around her shoulders. Maybe he could enjoy this part of the wake. Not the performing, because the knot in his gut had already started twisting. But being alone with Jolie in the dark, allowed to smell her hair... That could get him through this.

From somewhere behind the bleachers a spotlight popped on and focused on the ring. A white sheet hung on a frame—makeshift projection screen—and Granny Bohannon strolled up to the still blank screen. He'd always called her Granny, even if she wasn't his grandmother. A heart of gold and a mouth like a sailor in a small, spunky package. The Bohannon women all seemed to be as small as the Keightly men were large. "If Granny's the presenter for the evening, things are already looking up," Reece murmured, wanting her to enjoy things and not worry about his reaction. And it was true. Granny made everything either fun or utterly inappropriate. Usually both.

"She's been organizing the kids for this for weeks," Jolie whispered.

A slide appeared, one he recognized as the oldest in the collection. A very serious-looking performer without a smile. Once they'd gotten a good look at the picture, another spotlight came on, illuminating one of the kids in a replica of the old costume from the photo. The sandy-haired teen tried to juggle and ended up chasing the balls around the ring while Granny narrated...in language that almost made Reece blush.

He couldn't stop the smile that followed. "Start with

the clowns," he murmured to Jolie, who patted his arm again. They all loved to laugh. It was the best way to start off the wake. History, memories, and laughter. People he didn't know, people he did know, and some he wished he knew better.

The first non-clown performer to enter the ring had Reece tensing again. He squeezed her shoulders just a little too tight, not hurting her but making the turmoil he was feeling clear. Luckily, there was no rhyme or reason to the format of the wake. People had been preparing acts, tributes to the old acts from the past, compiling stories to tell and writing toasts. They took pride in every aspect, but there was no schedule or program.

Ten years ago, not equipped to know how to help him, Jolie now realized she'd failed to pick up on all his signals. Failed to help him through his father's death, or even recognize the kind of thoughts he'd been having. She'd thought she'd had him figured out, but if she had then he wouldn't be suffering now.

She'd lost her father too or, well, she'd been lost by her father, but the result had been similar. And she'd gotten over it. That's the only way to make it in life, get through the bad things until stuff got good again.

The sawdust had been a revelation. While she'd seen Reece's personality shift after his dad died, she'd always thought of it as being anger—that was the only emotion he'd ever allowed her to see until he'd made that unexpected sawdust confession.

The bright spotlights reflected off the sand and created a low glow in seats. Enough that she could see the muscle of his jaw bunching and the unnatural rise of his shoulders. But his biggest tell was the look of extreme concentration on his face. He didn't even seem aware that she was scrutinizing him.

Only an idiot wouldn't know he'd been in pain when his dad had died, but she just hadn't picked up on how traumatized he'd been until now.

"If I tell you a secret, do you promise not to tell anyone?" Jolie touched his hand again, trying to draw his attention from the ring.

"No," he replied, keeping tones low. "Maybe later." Because he was concentrating.

"No one is going to be hurt."

"Burns," Reece muttered. "Juggling seven clubs is just as impressive without fire or added danger."

"From a technical aspect, but it's not as exciting."

The look he gave her confirmed what she'd thought: He was escaping back into anger.

Armed with what she'd picked up this evening, Jolie now felt the need to protect Reece. To help him. Her own anger was still there, and still righteous—he had been an idiot to cut them all out of his life as he had done. And since he'd done it once, she had no doubt that he'd do it again, pack them all off at his earliest convenience. But she understood him a little better.

Her father leaving her had driven deep the need to stay within the safety of the circus, and his father dying had driven into Reece the idea that there was no safety at the circus.

Evening turned to night, then to morning. There were toasts, stories, and tributes. And no one got hurt. Reece met a new stepbrother, a fifteen-year-old boy called Anthony who'd come to Bohannon Farm as a ward of the state, part of their program to foster troubled kids. He endeared himself to Reece the instant he introduced himself and asked Reece and Jolie to come with him outside, and immediately bowed out with a slug to Reece's arm and a murmured, "You owe me."

"Did you put him up to that?" Jolie squinted at him, but mostly just looked amused.

Reece shook his head, smiling at Anthony's retreating back. "I did not. But I'm glad he picked up on my desire to escape." He offered a hand to Jolie and when she took it, he started walking toward the trailers.

They walked as close as they could, giving up hand-holding in favor of arms around each other. Before they even made it to the footpath leading to Jolie's trailer, they both knew where they were going. The question in Reece's mind was about whether or not she knew why he wanted to go there.

When she stepped up onto her stairs and turned to face him, the way she looked at his mouth for a few seconds before looking him in the eye was invitation enough.

He slipped his arms around her waist and closed his mouth over hers, kissing her with the longing he'd never lost.

Her soft lips parted in an instant, welcoming his tongue into her mouth.

The hands on his back squeezed, fingers pressing into the flesh in a way that caused a riot of goose-bumps and driving chills under the now dry material. No one else tasted like Jolie. No one else kissed like her either. She'd hold the kiss as long as he did, lack of oxygen be damned. When his heart had sped up to the point that he needed air, he broke the kiss but kept her close enough for them to fight for the same air with big shuddering breaths.

"This is a bad idea," Jolie whispered, swallowing and licking her kiss-swollen lips.

Reece shook his head. "Good idea."

"Bad idea. Bad bad…" She kissed him this time, re-leasing her hold on him to get at the jacket buttons and shed the bulky material that kept them apart. Freed from it, she pressed tight against him, the gauzy material of her dress leaving very little to his vivid imagination. God, he wanted to feel her. Everywhere.

CHAPTER FIVE

SHE PUSHED HER tongue into his mouth and he barely stifled a groan.

The groan made her pull away, or something did. She felt for the door behind her, flipping the latch and stepping to the side so she could swing the door open. "I don't know whether to invite you in."

"Invite me in. I...am a great guest." He grabbed his jacket and stepped up onto the stairs, which forced her up the remaining couple into the trailer.

"What I mean is I have rules. See, mostly I had one rule, but now I have four. I think. I might have five. Because..." She licked her lips and he closed the door, but couldn't take his eyes off the little pink tongue tracing her lips.

"I like rules." Reece would have said he liked anything at that point. The unfocused look of her eyes as she stared at his mouth made the words mostly meaningless anyway.

He dropped his jacket in the floor, wrapped his arms around her waist and lifted her against him.

No hesitation, she kissed him again, whatever she'd been trying to say. All heat, and deep kisses that made him question whether he'd have another episode like the last time they'd got heated.

The edge of the couch cushions touched the backs of his legs and Reece sat, arranging her legs to straddle his thighs as he leaned back, keeping her close so she could have no doubt how much he wanted her.

"I have rules." She tried again, winding her fingers in his hair and pulling to keep his head tugged back.

He couldn't tell whether the look in her eyes was the heat between them or an impending panic attack. The glazed sexiness was gone. "What rules?"

"Rules about men," she panted, shaking her head.

Freaking out was a sign to stop kissing her.

"I'm not sleeping with you." She blurted the words out before running them through her one-emotion-at-a-time rule. Lust was having a showdown with fear, and she couldn't decide which one to go with. Fear won for control of her mouth at that second.

"Okay." He reached up to pull her hands from his hair then carefully lifted her from his lap and placed her beside him on the couch. "Do you want me to leave?"

"I don't know." She could see both reactions as equally compelling.

Reece shifted, winced, and settled into the cushions again.

"Are you in pain?"

"I'm fine." He took a deep breath and looked at her. "I'd really like to know what you're thinking, though, because a minute ago...we were on the same wavelength. Then you started to panic."

"I'm still soggy."

Reece nodded. "So you want to change before we talk?"

It would give her a chance to think about what she could say to him, what information she was willing to part with... "Yes."

He gestured to the other end of the trailer. "I'll wait."

"Do you want to change too? I don't have much that would fit you, but you could go back to the RV and change."

"I'm not leaving. I want to talk and make sure you're all right. I'm making the most of our truce."

Jolie headed for the other side of the trailer and stripped down to her underwear with her back to him. There wasn't much privacy in the small living space, and she twisted to see if he was looking.

Of course he was looking. "Close your eyes."

"I've seen it all before."

"Do you really want to go there with me? I hear that rodeo riders can last at least eight seconds."

Reece winced.

That zinger had been a decade in the making. He looked away and she went back to changing. With clean underthings and her fluffy pink robe on, she wandered back to the couch, turned on a space heater on the way and sat down, feeling somewhat warmer if not more in control. She may not have changed that much since he'd last seen her, but he'd changed. It really wasn't fair.

"What's with the pink? You seem to wear it a lot now."

"I like pink. It's a myth that redheads can't wear pink." He looked large and out of place on her sofa. And something else, uncomfortable maybe. Angry? No, his jaw wasn't bunching, but he had that look of concentration again.

He looked her over and added, "You turn pink easier than you used to."

"One of the many ways I'm an enigma," she mumbled, and tried to remember why she'd stopped kissing him.

"Tell me your rule about men."

The color in his cheeks rose a little. "So you mean you don't date."

"I don't date," Jolie confirmed.

"How long has that been going on?"

She sighed. "Long enough. I don't need to date. And, honestly, there have been slim pickings with the circus.

We have guest artistes. Mom married one and is now travelling with a new circus family. But I haven't wanted to have to move on with a troupe when they left. So, no, I don't date. Though I am starting to see that I could now. I mean, if there is no need to be on the road any more then there isn't that obstacle when you're getting into a relationship. I don't really need anyone who is in the life any more." She didn't date, but right now she also didn't know how to get control of her mouth. He hadn't asked for all this information. "I'm not signing up for dating sites or whatever. I'm okay with not dating."

"You're not convincing me." He stretched back, keeping those blue eyes fixed on her. "No one who wants to be alone kisses the way you kissed me." He tilted his head in the direction of the big top. "You might be able to sell that line to someone else, but I have a very long memory."

It felt weird to talk about this. She'd gone so long without talking to anyone about these intimate details of her attempted love life, but Dr. Long Memory begged to be reminded. "Then you should remember how the sex went with us."

"I remember. Believe me. It's a dent in my ego that I'm the worst sex you ever had." The way she looked away from him and turned just a little pinker, a little guiltier meant something. "The only sex you ever had?"

She cleared her throat, shifting and straightening her robe so it kept her well covered. "That's not your business."

"The hell it's not if I put you off sex for life," Reece muttered, angrier than he rationally should be to hear those words. He certainly didn't want to hear that she'd been with, well, anyone else. But hearing that she'd been with no one since him...was worse. "You have no appetite for it?"

"I have a fine appetite, I just don't need a man to help me…with that."

"With orgasms, you mean." He tried to keep his mind blank, because this conversation had suddenly taken a new interesting turn and his mind summoned appropriate visuals.

"With orgasms," she confirmed with a grunt, waving a hand. "I don't need help. I can do it myself."

Definitely a mental image he could spend months contemplating…but not if he wanted to get anything else done. "There's m-more to it than that." He stammered, trying to find his cool. He'd had the idea that this conversation would help him understand her, and maybe help her somehow. Not break him.

"I have a toy and I'm not ashamed to say it."

More…fantastic mental images. Images that completely robbed him of words.

"So, however much better orgasms are with a penis, it's covered?"

Stop picturing. Stop, stop, stop.

He leaned forward, turned off the heater, and sat back again. He'd had a point to make… "Okay, but it's still different with someone."

"It's close enough. It can't be all that different." She squirmed around at the other end of the couch, growing pinker by the second, despite her claims. "The mechanics are all covered!"

"Oh, Jolie…you're either fooling yourself or trying to torture me." Maybe both.

The shake of her head that followed was slow, less certain than all this my-orgasms-are-acceptable-as-is talk had been.

"So you're saying that hypothetically, if someone else controlled the vibrator…"

"It doesn't vibrate." She waved a hand.

"So it's…"

"A kind of squishy penis thing."

Reece rubbed his face, trying to relax his brows before she gave him another headache. "So, hypothetically, by your definition if I controlled the…toy, it would be no different for you than doing it yourself." He should be trying to get this out of his mind, not grilling her about it. Only someone stupid would have this fight with her, but he needed her to know he was *right*. What kind of grown woman didn't understand this basic truth? The kind he'd broken.

"Right."

"Fibber. Please, tell me you don't really think that. You're just getting some payback because of how…awful I was the first time we…"

"If I was torturing you, I'd say, 'Here, hold my happy playtime-penis while I have an orgasm.' And afterward push you out the door. But that would be mean to you and meaningless to me."

"Fine."

"What?"

"Get your play…time…penis. Your whatever. Get it."

Jolie laughed, a breathy laugh that said she was picturing things now. "You're joking."

"No, I'm calling your bluff. You're just messing with me."

"Reece…"

"Say it, you're just—"

"I'm not messing with you! But sleeping together is a bad idea."

"You're right, I'm definitely not getting laid tonight. I don't have condoms with me, and unless you are lying about that rule against men in your life, you don't have them either."

"I don't have them."

"Then get your toy."

"Because you've seen it all before?"

"Because I've seen it, and you deserve to see me suffer after you know exactly what it means." A good man, knowing how she responded to dares, wouldn't dare her sexually. But he wasn't feeling like a good man right now. He was feeling like a very frustrated man who had to open her beautiful damned eyes. And maybe vindicate himself a little along the way.

"Is this what they taught you in Playing Doctor School? Because—"

"Hell, no. There will be nothing clinical about this. And I'm still of the mind that it would be insanely hot, but if you want to turn me off the idea fast, keep up the doctor talk. Makes it smarmy and unappea…less appealing."

Jolie watched his face, and then she pointedly looked at his groin. Yeah, he might just suffer from this if she agreed to it. "So you are swearing you won't try to have sex with me."

"I promise you, I will behave myself."

She considered a moment. Pros and cons. Pro: she would get to make him suffer. He'd taken her virginity and then promptly freaked out, had got out of there and run away—like to another freaking state and never came back. Making him suffer and give her an orgasm? That sounded vaguely like justice. Pervy poetic justice…if she didn't have some kind of performance issue. Did women get those? And he would have nothing and suffer and… she wasn't sleeping with him. No matter what he said… and he could be made to want something really bad and not have it. *Like her camp.*

Cons: he might break his promise. He did have a record of broken promises, and he was right about there being no condoms in the house. Which could mean that there might be a little Bohannon in her future. Which actually wouldn't be a con. She loved kids. She just didn't love the idea of being abandoned by a lover or husband or a whatever Reece was.

Too many emotions to think about, especially when the big one that kept distracting her was the idea of more kissing... One emotion at a time.

"Fine. But you should know that I have no good and honorable motives. And no matter how much you want to have sex after, I'm not going to do it. I'm not going to touch your penis. I'm not going to kiss it or anything else. And oral sex seems dangerous. I'm not doing it."

"I wouldn't ask. This is all about me proving I'm right." He stood up, grabbed her off the couch, and marched the short distance toward the bedroom. "But you're going to have to explain the 'dangerous' comment later."

"I know how that thing goes off willy-nilly, like an unstable grenade. And if it's by my face...I would really have to insist on some kind of protective eyewear. Goggles."

"That was one time," Reece muttered, and now had the mental image of her with goggles on, and it was still sexy to him. God, he should put a halt to this nonsense.

"You really have to stop picking me up and carting me around. You're not a caveman. Didn't they teach you any vocabulary at doctor school?"

"Medical school," he corrected again, since he was pretty sure she was calling it doctor school now to annoy him. "I know a lot of big words. You don't want to play Scrabble with me. I dominate."

"I imagine if your opponent gets the letters you want, you just pick them up and move them where you want them to go."

"Don't you?" He put her down at the foot of the bed and began shedding clothes. Probably looked like he wanted to get this over with, and he kind of did...but it was more eagerness. She'd made him stop looking earlier. "Why are you just sitting there? Get the toy. Does it have a name?"

"No. Of course not." She gestured to the bedside table while looking him over. He wouldn't stop her. The point of this completely insane idea was to show her that sex was better with a partner, not a toy.

The way she looked up at him was an encouragement until she said, "Leave the boxers on."

Getting undressed was a little harder for Jolie. Reece stripped without a shred of hesitation, but she couldn't match that. Her boldness almost abandoned her as she reached for her panties and stopped to look at him.

This wasn't the sort of thing she'd ever have pictured herself doing on a dare. But if she was honest, that wasn't all this was. She had his taste still on her lips, and the memory of his warm hand in hers. The idea of being flesh to flesh with him—of feeling the length of his big body melding against hers—awakened a need inside her she'd not felt in a long time.

And she knew he was right there with her. His pupils dilated, his mouth was open, and there was a color on his cheeks she would have called exertion in any other circumstances...they all added up to the same thing. It may have been ten years, his face might have changed, matured, but she could still recognize want in him. He still wanted her. Logically, she knew he'd probably shared that look with a number of other women since he'd left her. And tomorrow she'd no doubt remember that...but right now he wanted her. Not anyone else. She deserved a night of that. Whether or not he deserved to suffer, she couldn't really say.

"Come here." He held out one hand and when she took it and sat on the bed, topless beside him, he guided her mouth back to his.

Something else to think about tomorrow, when she'd probably regret this. Right now she was stuck in some loop of not believing him, wondering if he was right, wanting him to be right, and then wondering if she'd regret finding out.

His breath came fast, and her heart sped up in tandem. Probably some primitive warning system she'd also regret ignoring.

She shut it down. The way his hands gripped and squeezed, greedy for the feel of her, that peculiar trembling low in her belly...all shouted a little louder than that warning system.

They stretched out on the bed, and when the hair on his chest teased her flesh, she was surprised to find her breasts beginning to ache. Kissing had been a great deal calmer when they'd first started doing it. And by the time they'd got around to it affecting her breasts, eager hands had been involved, and sometimes his mouth. But he hadn't even touched them yet, and her body was already responding.

She slid her hands to his head and curled her fingers in his longish sandy locks, pulling his head away. Air, she needed air. Her heart was beating too hard and too fast. As soon as their lips parted she took several great shuddering breaths, all the while staring into eyes as blue as a stormy sea.

He would break his promise. That's what Reece did. The muscles in his arms and back strained and shook with restraint, but it wouldn't last. He'd at least try to break his promise. For the first time she was fairly certain she'd let him.

She closed her eyes, trying to calm down, trying to still her hips and belly, which alternated between writhing into the mattress and quivering. The sensation of his warm hand tracking up the inside her thigh got her eyes open again. "That's not Mr. Happy."

He grinned as she spilled the name of her toy. "I'll get you for the lie later." His smile faded and he just watched her eyes. "Just want to make sure…you're ready."

A tremor of anticipation started deep inside her, and every whiffled breath confirmed for him before his long fingers found her sex and gave a long stroke.

Pleasure lanced through her, and somewhere in the back of her mind Jolie was aware she was supposed to compare this with pleasure she'd had on her own. But thinking was entirely too much effort.

Reece's look of concentration returned, and with it high, tight breaths. If her horses ground their teeth like he was doing, she'd bit them. Okay, yes, he was suffering. She couldn't even take any pleasure in that because the terrible need coiled in her felt like suffering too. It had never been this intense, even compared to how awful it had been that one other time they'd started to make love and he'd…had issues and bailed immediately afterward.

He licked his lips, withdrew his had hand from between her legs, and the fingers that had stroked her went into his mouth, shocking every other thought from her mind. She became aware that he was proceeding with the imitation penis when she felt it gliding, seeking her entry.

His eyes devoured her. She knew before he'd even slid the toy home that it was going to be the best orgasm she'd ever had. No doubt lingered that one waited for her. But she was supposed to do her part too…and slid a hand toward her sex.

Reece let go of the toy, grabbed and pinned her hands above her head.

"What are you—?"

"I'm the one who gets to." He crossed her arms at the wrists and held them with one hand, the other sliding back to the toy and beginning to move it. In and out, slow then fast, twisting and straight, adjusting the angle by the sounds every lick of pleasure ripped from her. But it wasn't enough. Just a pathetic substitute for what she desperately wanted. She wanted to feel the heat of him between her legs, feel the muscles on his back flex as he moved inside her…and she wanted him to feel. Pleasure. And whatever that dark current passing between them even now was…she knew it'd be more.

"Take it away." She panted the words, unable to move her hands and do it herself. The distress in her voice must have reached him. He stopped, breathing as hard as she, and shook his head, confused.

"I want you. I don't want it. I want you." She nodded, backing up her shameless, desperate words.

Reece closed his eyes, shook his head and began slowly working it within her again. "I promised." His hand still held hers, wound together now more than pinned. He opened his eyes and watched her. "I can feel you shaking. Don't fight it. You need it. I need it."

Then he whispered, "I will never break another promise to you, Jolie, no matter what it costs me."

It wasn't true… She'd never be that important to anyone. But the fantasy of it pushed her over the edge. When her climax came, her body bucked, but she kept her head still and her eyes locked to his. He knew she didn't believe him. She could see it in the frown that flashed through his eyes. No barriers existed between them right now.

She'd have expected him to gloat, but there wasn't even a hint of victory in his tortured gaze. He said nothing to taunt her, no *I told you so.*

He simply withdrew the toy, his hand shaking as he laid it behind him on the bed, and dragged her whatever fraction of an inch she was away from him—not satisfied until their flesh melded and his arms held her. Burying his face in her hair and his nose in the nape of her neck, he shuddered and sighed.

Stiff and unyielding, his erection pressed against the cleft of her butt, but he did nothing to relieve himself. Just held her while both their hearts tried to slow back down.

Jolie was the first one to crack. However much she wanted to punish him for the past decade, now she just wanted him to feel what she'd felt. "I could touch you..."

"No. I told you. I'm not going to break any more promises to you. Not now, not ever." He shuddered again, but apparently deciding that he couldn't stay tucked against her warmth he released her and rolled to his back and then to a sitting position at the foot of the bed and reached for his pants.

"You're leaving?"

"I'm removing myself from temptation." He tugged the pants on as he stood, and wrested them over the...impressive tent in his tight boxers.

She hadn't taken the time to admire him before, but he really had stayed in magnificent form in his time away from the circus. "You were right," she whispered, unable to keep from an honorable answer when he was suffering to keep from breaking promises.

"We can talk about that tomorrow." He pulled his shirt on, in a hurry to get out of there, but he did pause to look at her. "Are you okay?" He smiled, a tired, forced grin if she'd ever seen one.

Jolie nodded, pulling the sheet over herself as much for him as for her.

Reece stepped around the bed, bent down and kissed her on the head, then made his way to the door. It closed and she scooted into the warm spot he'd left on her bed and pulled the blankets over her to keep what little of his heat remained.

She should try to figure out what this meant before they

talked about it. But if he remained true to form, he'd beat feet and she'd see him when he came to sell the equipment to some buyer.

Knocking at the door and the sound of his name being called in a frantic manner pulled Reece from fitful sleep. He stumbled out of bed and to the door, then wrenched it open to find Granny Bohannon there, looking wild-eyed.

"Get your doctor things. One of my boys got hurt."

It had been a few months since his last ER rotation, but he shook his sleepiness out and focused. "Hurt how?"

"Fell, got his arm bent around bad somehow. Don't know if it's broke, but we can't hardly get him on his feet. Dammit. I told him to stay the hell off the equipment, but he listens about as good as my fifth husband. And he was the deafest son of a..."

Another bone injury? Reece left Granny cussing at the door, crammed his feet into his shoes, grabbed the bag he'd brought with him for the exams he planned on offering today, and took off out the door behind her. She'd already climbed onto a four-wheeler and gunned the engine, leaving him the seat behind. And she hadn't stopped complaining in a vocabulary blue enough to make high-school boys jealous.

And just what his ego needed: to hold onto a tiny ninety-year-old woman to keep from being dumped off the back of an ATV. He stuck his arm through the handle on his bag and reached behind himself to grab a metal rack in the hope it would save him from an unexpected head injury.

They bounced over the uneven ground, which turned out to be as good as coffee when trying to wake up from staying up all night, staring down the gullet of the beast from your past that kept trying to swallow you whole, and then volunteering for more sexual frustration than he could have imagined before Jolie and her toy...

It didn't take long to reach the barn, it just felt like it. Reece got off when Granny rolled the vehicle to a stop, and followed an especially sober-looking teen into the barn where several people were gathered around boy of about fifteen, leaning against a post, his face ashen from pain.

Jolie knelt beside the boy, helping hold his arm to his chest for stability. So they had gone to her first? Seemed they weren't entirely ready to take what he was offering yet, but at least they had when Jolie presumably hadn't been able to help.

She looked at him long enough to confirm where her thoughts were too. The blush just added to his awareness and difficulty in focusing.

"His shoulder is dislocated," she announced, keeping the arm held in place and shifting her gaze back to the kid. "Anterior dislocation of the humerus."

Reece stooped beside the boy. "How can you tell?" he asked, but a quick examination confirmed Jolie's diagnosis.

"Well, it's in front of where it's supposed to be. Probably hit it on the back as he fell because the ball is in front of the socket." Jolie pointed to a bump that shouldn't have been there. "If it were worse, like a sprain or a break, there'd probably be lots of swelling and bruising by now." She reached up to push her hair back from her face, looking back at Sam and offering the teen a tight smile.

"Good instincts."

"I've had some experience with this type of injury," she murmured, deflecting the praise.

"You've had a dislocated shoulder?"

She nodded but didn't look at him. Because the circus life was dangerous, no matter how much she'd like to pretend otherwise. Right. He could deal with this later.

"Bet that hurts." He shifted his attention to the boy, whose breathing sped up as Reece pulled his arm from the protective fold across his chest and began moving it slightly. Scared, anticipating pain.

Jolie moved around and knelt on the other side of the kid. "Look at me, Sam. Hurts like crazy, I know. And it's about to hurt a lot more for just like…a few seconds. Imagine you're putting all that pain into a ball, and we're going to kick it away. That kick is going to hurt…but then it's going to be gone. Yeah, it's really going to suck, but after it's going to feel so much better. You need to relax and do what Reece says to make that happen. Can you do that?"

So much for his usual plan, which was to say, "You might feel some discomfort…"

"I'll try," the kid said.

"Just keep looking at me," Jolie said, one hand on the boy's cheek to keep him face to face with her.

The muscles liked to spasm when the bones were out of the socket like this, and he'd only ever set an anterior dislocation once, but he remembered how to do it. With the boy sitting there on the dirt floor, his gaze fixed on Jolie's, Reece slowly lifted and rotated the arm, drawing a scream from the kid but causing the head of the humerus to reseat itself.

Jolie winced, but the scream—like the pain—passed fast, as she had promised. Just not before the boy had jerked away from her, leaned to the side and thrown up his breakfast. Or lunch. It was later than Reece had thought when Granny had come banging on his door.

"Breathe, Sam. It's all over." She leaned away from the vomit and stood pretty quickly.

Granny held out a bottle of water to Reece. He smiled at her, uncapped it and handed to the boy. "It's okay, Sam. Natural reaction to extreme pain." He wrapped an arm around the boy's middle and hauled him back from the barf, then pressed the water bottle into his hand. "Drink this. It'll help."

A few seconds later, while they all stared at the kid, the color started coming back to his face.

"Feel better?" Reece asked.

A nod, and he held the water to Jolie so he could use his hands to stand up. Not wanting him to use his newly reduced arm, Reece slung an arm around his waist and helped him stand. "Bet the next time Granny says don't climb on the equipment…"

"I won't," Sam filled in, then muttered, "I'd really like to lay down."

"I'll go fetch the golf cart," Granny announced, and pointed to a chair. "Sit. I'll be right back."

Sam obeyed.

"If you have a sling at the house, or some material we can fake one with, that'd be good too, Granny," Reece called after her.

She waved. He hoped that meant she understood.

Jolie hovered around the kid, and Reece gave them both the necessary aftercare instructions. He couldn't trust the kid to remember, but Jolie really did have a head for this stuff, terminology or no.

"You're good with the kids," he commented, and soon Granny returned with a sling and got them all onto the golf cart for a ride to the big house. Sam sat in the front, and he and Jolie sat in the back with their legs dangling off the vehicle—hers dangled better. He had to work to keep his feet off the ground.

She reached behind him and slid a box from behind him to behind her, allowing him to scoot back enough to keep his feet from banging on the ground.

"I like the kids," Jolie answered finally. "They've been kicked around by the outside world too. It helps them to be here with us."

She really didn't like the outside world.

"But you probably see that kind of thing all the time," Jolie said, hopping off the back of the cart as Granny rolled it to a stop. "You can get callous about that kind of thing. Probably doesn't bother you much any more, right? You see it every day, you get used to it."

She smelled good. His libido, never really normal since the night before, kicked in—memories of her squirming beneath his touch and the disheveled bed steeped in her sweet scent... He couldn't think, and she was probably saying something important to him. Reece stood and turned to grab his bag, and in doing so he saw several of the company members waiting on the big wraparound porch.

"We're here to see the doctor," someone said, taking Reece's attention off Jolie. He counted...eight new patients waiting.

"Got a place set up inside. Used to be a laundry room before we set up the laundry in the pole barn there," Granny announced, but she stuck by the kid, pointed to some building, and gestured for Reece to follow her inside.

When he looked back to tell Jolie he wanted to talk to her later, she was already far enough away that he'd have had to shout for her to hear him.

Later. He'd find her later. Right now he had a family to take care of, and for the first time since he'd come back into their lives, Reece felt like he was doing his job.

A good feeling that would have to hold him through being the village hard-ass again later when he told Jolie no to the camp idea and wrecked the connections they'd reforged yesterday and last night.

But a truce could only last so long.

CHAPTER SIX

AFTER THE LONG task of compiling medical histories for the last generation of performers, and with the extensive list of their profession-related health problems in mind, Reece went in search of Jolie. He still had a couple to see after they got done with the day's chores, but there was a break he could take advantage of now.

If the wake had given him any doubts about his decision, the twisted spines and cartilage-free joints shared by every performer he'd seen so far shored up those doubts.

He found Jolie by following the music to the big top, where she was perched on a wire strung between two portable stands, not exactly a high wire but a good ten feet off the ground.

The leather slippers she wore he recognized from seeing other wire dancers, but the hand guards protecting her palms were new to him.

A slow, sultry guitar solo blared from hidden speakers, but the music paused as she slid her front foot forward on the wire. She looked toward the player, lost her balance and fell.

Reece started forward, and had run several yards down the causeway when he realized she wasn't on the ground— or on the mats below. Thank God she had mats down.

Ever nimble in reflexes, she'd managed to catch the wire on the way and was now pulling herself back up.

Maybe that's what the hand guards were for. The thing bowed and stretched some where her hands put pressure, but she managed to get back on it and onto her feet.

With a few quick, bouncing steps she ran the length of the wire to one of the towers, bent over, grabbed a remote, started the song over again, and approached the wire again.

It was a routine. She was practicing a routine...what other reason would she have for starting the music over? The mats and his curiosity gave him the strength to stand and watch her, when otherwise all he wanted to do was make her get down onto solid ground where she couldn't fall to her death.

Her moves started slow and sinuous, the kind of moves he'd expect in a belly dance or a strip tease. Sexy didn't fly in American circuses, but if she could move like that, she might pull it off. Maybe in Vegas...not that she belonged in Vegas.

Reece stuck to the shadows to keep from interrupting her, but he did stand out enough to look around and see if anyone else was watching.

Just when his thoughts started to scrape bottom, the music picked up and she began a series of heart-stopping leaps, feet high off and back low on the wire. Within the space of a few notes she'd gone from siren on the high wire to something that he'd expect to see in gymnastics. Some combination of beam and bar that at once thrilled and terrified him.

If she fell she'd land on the mats. He repeated the mantra every time his heart stopped.

Now he understood what the hand guards were for—to protect her palms when she swung on that wire. Not just safety gear should she fall.

She let go of the wire three times during different spins and angles. The final one she didn't catch but used it to dismount, and he had never been so thankful for mats in his life.

Another new experience: being both terrified and turned on at the same time. And neither of those reactions did he particularly want to admit to.

The only thing he could admit to right now? She was still a performer—as much as pained him to admit it. She had to want to, no one kept in that kind of conditioning if they didn't want to.

Well, no one but him. He didn't want to perform, but he still wanted to be in the kind of shape he'd have been if he hadn't left. It was part of the life...just how he'd been raised, to value the peak of human performance that highly. If she didn't have an actual routine choreographed with music, he might be able to believe that was her reason too. But it felt more like something else he'd broken when he'd left.

Maybe her wish for the camp was a way to try and satisfy that need. Even believing herself alone in the big top, she smiled. She glowed, though the siren-like quality to her performance was new.

"I thought you'd have interrupted," Jolie said, unwrapping the guards from her wrists and turning to look toward where Reece skulked in the shadows. "Really didn't expect to get to the releases."

"I didn't think you saw me." Reece stepped out of the shadows and immediately took a seat on the raised outside edge of the ring. "The music pause makes you stumble, but you go jumping and leaping and don't get dizzy? Makes no sense."

"I don't know why. I think I have an inner-ear condition."

Reece focused then, brows pinched.

"I'm kidding." Jolie laughed, hanging the guards over

one of the rungs on the tripod ladders up to the wire. "I really don't know the answer. I couldn't at first, but I was convinced it was possible...so I just kept trying. Eventually it got easier."

"I read something about ballet dancers training their brains to ignore the inner-ear signals of dizziness. Maybe it's something like that," Reece said, but he still looked a little freaked out. And tense. "Speaking of conditions, how's your arm?"

"Smooth segue." Jolie stopped beside him and sat. "A little sore but manageable."

"You should get it X-rayed." He reached for her arm and ran the pad of his thumb over the remnants of the bite, a gentle touch that sent a wash of goose-bumps up her arm and down over her chest. Her breasts reacted, small as they were, and she suddenly became hyper-aware of the leotard stretched across the sensitive peaks.

He noticed. And then he made a point of looking at the wire. "The dance...the act? Very sexy. When you weren't flipping around, scaring the hell out of me."

"I had the mats down for safety. And I toned down the sexiness a lot. It's hard to play with those emotions for no one."

"I wouldn't say no one. You knew I was here."

"I also knew you'd freak if I performed for you, and what might that do to my concentration?" She grinned and drew her arm back from his inspecting gaze. "You look like you have something on your mind."

Reece nodded, a smile saved for her. "I do. I'm just blown away a little." He looked at her mouth just long enough to prepare her. "And I decided there was something else I'd rather do than talk."

Jolie swallowed just before his mouth came down on hers and his arms went around her, lifting her from the seat as he stood and covering the short distance to lay her on the oversized mats beneath her wire, pinning her and rousing her recently super-charged passion.

Kissing could happen without promises to stay forever. He wouldn't stay forever, she knew that. He'd leave her again, and them having kissed or having gone to bed together wouldn't matter to him at all when he made the decision to go.

She wouldn't let it go too far. She would stop before her brain entirely turned into hormone pudding.

In a little while…

Nap time. Some people might think the smell of the stables to be the sort of thing you didn't want to sleep with, but Jolie disagreed. None of the horses were allowed to trample in their filth. The stalls were kept clean and as fresh as could be. The strongest scent was the hay, except for right after the horses came in sweaty. There was that odor too. But as hot as it had gotten this week, no one was up to getting themselves or the horses sweaty. Least of all her.

So, naturally, someone would be walking around in the stable, interrupting her nap time. Jolie knew who it was before she opened her eyes. "Reece." She lifted the sleep mask she liked for her stable napping and looked at the massive man looking down at her from the head of her cot. "Seriously, when did you get so big? Big as a horse. I could ride you." She paused, pulled her mask off and sat up, like that would make her not say stupid things. "Okay, that came out wrong."

He smiled. "I could throw you over my shoulder. I know how you like being carried around."

"Oh, yeah, every woman wants her butt in the air for the world to see." She swung her legs off the edge of the cot and reached for her boots. "What can I do for you?"

Reece tilted his head behind him to the many full-sized mounts in their stalls. "Thought we could go for a ride."

"You're here in the middle of the week. That's a new one for you. Sounds like something more than a horseback ride."

He nodded. "We should talk."

It was her turn to nod. "And you think we'll talk better on horseback? Because that seems like a distraction, some kind of sleight of hand to try and distract me from something that you don't want to say."

"Not entirely wrong, but it would also be nice to get out in the fresh air." Reece stepped back from the stall and held the door for her. "I also wanted to check on Gordy." The small horse was sleeping again. "Did you stop his tranquilizers?"

When Jolie stepped out of the stall, he went back in and squatted down to look at the cast holding the horse's leg in place.

This stall was bigger than the ones in the traveling stable, but Reece took up enough room for her to give him the space. She stayed in the doorway watching him. "I stopped his tranquilizers. But he still has some pain medicine and I occasionally give him a mild sedative just to keep him mellow. I don't know if he actually needs them, his mood is pretty good, but I imagine it keeps him from trying to walk around too much. Every now and then he kicks his back legs and tries to buck out of the sling, but the one the vet brought is good. He gives up pretty quick."

"Still on poop vigil?"

"Nope, his belly is doing just fine. The kids are cleaning the stall frequently. Especially since they keep sneaking him apples."

"I was going to ask you about the kids. How many are there?" Reece backed out of the stall and closed the door, taking over in his bossy manner.

Since she had pointed out his reason for asking her to go for a ride, he was now using another method to distract her. "Seven." She cleared her throat and dropped her hands to her hips, planting herself in his path.

"I don't want to go riding. I'm tired. I'm sore. It's hot. I'm borderline cranky. And I'm pretty sure you came here to tell me something I don't want to hear, which I guess I should be grateful for—the fact that you're willing to at least tell me bad news in person."

"Jo..." He stopped her tirade with one syllable, and when she stood staring at him, waiting for him to spit it out, he sighed and gestured her to a bench.

"I don't want to sit. Is that how they taught you to break the bad news to people in doctor school?"

"Medical school," Reece corrected, an edge coming into his voice that said the cool look he wore was more fragile than he'd like it to be. "I want you to sit down so you don't feel like I'm looming over you. I want to talk to you, not intimidate you. That's easier if we're closer to eye level."

"I don't think that's going to help us see eye to eye."

"Stop." He reached for her, like he was going to pick her up and put her on the bench, but then caught himself and drew back again. Old habits did die hard. "Fine. I'll sit. You can stand."

Jolie folded her arms over her chest and looked at him, a little more irritated that his sitting did make him look less intimidating. "I'll stand." And those few inches she had on him in height then would help...

"I am not able to support your camp idea," he said without further preamble. Right to the heart of his decision. "It's not safe. I understand why you want to do it, and I appreciate you wanting to keep Keightly intact, take care of everyone, but it's not the way."

"Because you don't think I can do it."

"I honestly don't know if you could do it, but that isn't why I've come to this conclusion." He frowned, wearing the serious expression she assumed was supposed to show how tortured he was about these hard decisions he had to come to for the greater good…and the idiots who couldn't take care of themselves. "You might manage it just fine, though I have doubts considering how you avoid leaving the safety of the farm. But the real issue is the danger. Someone would get hurt. Add to that what a waste of your talent it would be."

Talent. Right. This was about what was best for her. The man was a walking contradiction. "I'm sorry, is this that thing you do to break bad news to people by saying something good with the something bad so that they don't feel like the bad thing is as bad?"

"No." Reece leaned against the wall behind the bench, watching her in a way that made the height difference no longer matter. "You want to be performing."

"I don't want to be performing," Jolie grunted. "I want to be here, with my family. I want to take care of them. I want to preserve our traditions and our way of life. We can do that here without being on the road." Okay, she did enjoy performing, but that wasn't the biggest part of her life. They were. Even if Reece didn't care about any of that any more.

"You aren't being honest with yourself. You haven't seen yourself perform. You glow. It was always your dream. Didn't change, did it?"

"It changed. I was sixteen. It's not my dream any more. My dream…" What was her dream? The camp. And, well… "My dream is for everything to stay the way it was. But that isn't going to happen. So now my dream is doing the best that I can for everyone. And the camp is a good idea. No, it's a great idea. You think everyone is just going to settle down and retire, but that's not who these people are. They want to do this, but they're going to listen to what you say and not put up a fuss. Because when they look at you they see Henry Keightly, the boss, a man who everyone loved and respected, and who did everything for this family. I look at you and I see...broken promises and control issues."

"Broken promises?" Reece scowled, his own arms crossing now so that they stared over their arms at one another. "You see more than that. What word have I broken lately?"

"Having a good track record for a couple of weeks doesn't wipe out the bad one you've had for a decade. I'm not stupid, I know that you are here now and you'll act fully present and connected to everyone, but as soon as you decide to go somewhere else, you'll go without a backward glance. I remember that part of you very well. Do you want me to tell you what it was like? Because I can tell you—in excruciating detail—just how long it took me to give up on you."

He didn't say anything, but his nostrils flared and his lips compressed. Nothing to say? Well, she had plenty!

"You haven't been willing to have any of us in your life until you thought you could come in here and control us, unless we do what you say we can't be part of your life. That's how it is. That's probably why you became a doctor, so people would pay you to tell them what to do."

"That's not true." Reece spoke quietly, and she remembered that voice. She got louder and louder the angrier she got, but Reece got quieter. "I'm buying a practice fifteen minutes from here and making this place my home."

"And everyone here is going to listen to your orders. Except me. So, what's the solution? Get me to go find some other circus to join, because obviously I should be performing! Should I be offended that you're worried about the safety of everyone but me, who obviously should be performing?"

"Jolie, I'm trying to take care of everyone and do right

by them. And doing right by you doesn't fit into the plan of what's right for everyone else. You're different. And stop saying 'obviously'. I hate it when you say that, like anything about you is obvious. Ever."

"I'm just so darned different..."

"Stop," he ordered again, then changed direction on her. "You know how much all the equipment is worth? I have a buyer. It will endow the farm for a long time, take care of the animals, and the people who take care of the animals will have a wage. It's a lot of money."

"The camp would bring in money too, and allow everyone here to hold onto their pride rather than being put out to pasture."

"You're not thinking clearly. You're just too emotional about this. No one is putting anyone out to pasture." He gritted his teeth—that muscle in the corner of his jaw bunching in time with her rapid heartbeat. "Your dream is for everything to stay like it was? That way you don't have to go out into the world and be part of it. You want this camp so you can still be in the life without actually being in the life. No ties outside the circus. No learning to get along with regular people."

"Are you joking? I'm talking about inviting strangers into my home on a daily basis, forever. I'm talking about pulling back the curtain and showing children that the magic isn't magic. That they can do great things if they work at it, no matter what anyone out there says about them." She knew that world very well, and she knew exactly why she had to stay away from it. "I'm going to do this, no matter what you say."

"Are you?" He stood up again. Sitting no longer worked for him. Or he had decided he needed to be more intimidating to make her agree.

Jolie squinted, not feeling intimidated so much as empowered by finally getting to have the fight with him that she should have had years ago. She stormed up to him, stepped to the side, and then right up onto the bench he'd vacated, forcing him to turn around to keep that intimidating stare. Unfortunately, that also put him in primo chest-poking range, and she was fired up enough that her index finger was already rod-straight and itching to jab him in his impressive torso.

"I know what I'm doing this week. Going to the bank! They give business loans and I'm smart enough to figure out how to get one for this. Though, honestly, with all the supporters we have, if the loan is troublesome I am certain I could finance the camp by contacting a few of Keightly's former supporters. Then I'll buy the equipment from someone lest prone to tyranny than you are. It won't have the Keightly name but the Bohannons are known too. I can keep the Keightly name off everything so your family legacy isn't sullied by my ineptitude. It would have been good for advertising, and to have the iconic tent for the children to perform in, but there are trapeze schools who set up outside, and the free-standing rigging isn't all that expensive."

He didn't flinch from her bench, and to his credit he didn't grab her and put her back on the ground either. He stood his ground, arms still crossed, though his thumbs stuck out in that annoying he-man manner that made her want to bend them backwards.

"So you're just going to stick a sign up by the highway and hope people come? You know if you really want to do this you will have to go to schools to introduce the idea, talk to parents at activities and athletics centers and let people know what's going on. Get insurance for everything—"

"I'm not a shut-in, Reece. I do go out when I need to. I speak the language and everything! I may not like it out there, but I can do it. You act like I'm asking you for charity. I'm offering you the chance to honor two hundred years of history in a venture that *makes money*. Not just uses it up."

"You don't understand how much responsibility this is. And, yes, it might make great wads of money, but this equipment is mine and even if I do nothing for this camp besides supply equipment, at the end of the day it's my responsibility if anyone gets hurt." His voice rose. Finally she'd struck a nerve.

"Fine, then it's settled. I'll get the equipment somewhere else. Go ahead and sell off the big top."

He loosed a loud groan of frustration and turned to walk away from her, enough to presumably give him room to get hold of his hands if they reached out to grab her again. "You remember how it was when Dad died. You remember how awful it was. I know you do. For God's sake, Gordy's hurt because he's a working animal. And we've had a number of really close calls with other performers in the past. Some who were injured badly enough they couldn't perform any more. You don't want to saddle children with that, Jolie. You ignore the danger. Have you seen how many of them have back and bad joint problems?"

"I'm not ignoring the danger, I'm just not going to be crippled by it."

"No, you let yourself be crippled by other things."

She took a breath and forced herself to stop for a few seconds, think about what he was saying. Was that an acknowledgment that he was crippled by the fear of other people dying like his dad had? "You want me to say I have abandonment issues? Fine. I do. I also don't want to go out there and get a job in an office and have a house with a white picket fence, live in a subdivision where it is supposed to look like a community but where everyone's interaction ends at their property line."

"What's so bad about it?"

"Loneliness is a sickness, Reece. People medicate it with materialism and they forget the things that are important."

"There are worse things than being alone."

Her face suddenly felt cold and she knew the angry red face she'd worked up had abandoned her. Jolie could hardly believe he'd just said that to her. "No, there isn't." She'd never say to him that there were worse things than watching your dad die in a horrific accident. Her throat constricted, but it was the burning in her eyes that demanded she summon her anger again. Anger was better than tears. "If you think telling me all the ways that it's too hard for me will do anything but make me more resolved than ever, then you've done a really good job of forgetting everything you ever knew about me. But thank you for reminding me for the thing I forgot about you."

"What's that? That I'm always right?"

"No, that it's stupid to get into bed with Reece Keightly, because the sting lasts longer than he does!"

Done with this conversation, with hoping that he'd do the right thing, Jolie stepped down and stormed toward the door.

"What are you doing?"

"Leaving!" she answered, but didn't turn round. She just raised her voice to make sure he could hear her. Strategic yelling. "I'd think that would be something you'd recognize when you saw it."

Reece watched Jolie leave, the wind knocked out of him as effectively as a punch to the solar plexus. He took a few steps back and sat on the bench again.

Because it turned out that shaming himself for taking her virginity in that way was one thing, and having her say it out loud were wildly different things.

Jolie had more reason than anyone in the world to hold

grudges against him, but she still kept trying to be kind and generous with him. She had taken care of the sawdust for him. Had put down the mats below her wire so he'd be more at ease. Tried to preserve his family history and the Keightly dynasty...but there was still a wound there.

A big one.

She was right to question his staying power.

She was also right that he was a control freak. Letting her buy the equipment and do this without his support—or his input—with his people... At least if he let her use the Keightly equipment and the name, he could keep some constraints on what was taught at the camp. Establish a curriculum that would minimize the possibility that she'd have massive future regrets. Make sure he did the physicals so that the kids were all healthy enough to participate...

He groaned, and then got up and went into Gordy's stall to sit with the little horse, who was actually awake and eating. He did look better. He'd been ready to give up on the little stallion in those first days, but Jolie had stuck it out. She didn't let go of anything she loved without a fight. Which made him wonder: had she ever actually let go of him? He'd denied her the fight. Denied her the closure.

He should go back to his apartment and get ready for work tomorrow. This week and next, Dr. Richards was overseeing him treating his patients. There was no contractual clause demanding that, but Richards wanted that extra bit of reassurance that his people would be in good hands, and Reece could understand that. He felt the same way and wanted Richards to be at ease with the transition and the future care of his people.

Even if the core company no longer bore the Keightly stamp in any form, even if they lived on the Bohannon farm, he'd consider every one of them to be his people until the very end.

* * *

"I'm here to see Reece."

Reece knew that voice. He followed Richards into the exam room, and smiled as soon as he saw the patient. "Anthony, this is Dr Richards, he built this practice."

Anthony introduced himself as Reece's brother, extending his hand. When Richards appeared confused, Reece jumped in and explained about how Anthony had come to be his new stepbrother.

"Could I just see Reece? I have a problem that I would rather…"

"Certainly." Richards nodded and left the room.

When the door closed, Reece rolled a stool over to where Anthony sat and joined him. "Are you worried about Granny? Or are you here for yourself?" Please, don't let the girlfriend be pregnant… Jolie already gave him too much Bohannon drama to deal with.

"I'm here for me." Anthony took a deep breath. "I didn't want to tell Mack and Ginny. Didn't want to tell anyone really. But now I think I have to."

"Well, whatever you say to me as a doctor, I will keep in confidence." Reece maybe shouldn't see his own stepbrother as a patient, but he'd do it this once to find out what was wrong, if nothing else.

"I'm diabetic. Type II. I used to be pretty big, you know, chubby…when I was a kid, before you guys took me in, and then I got diabetes. But as I got older, I lost weight, it got better. I didn't have to take medicine for it any more, so I didn't think I needed to tell anyone about it." His knees bounced in the seat and he looked down a lot.

Reece took the hint to help him out. "But something has changed?"

"I've been using Granny Bohannon's meter to check my blood sugar every day. She knows about my diabetes, but I didn't want to tell anyone else. I didn't think it was important any more."

He could read between the lines: Anthony thought Mack wouldn't adopt him if he knew he had an illness. Reece understood hiding weaknesses. He nudged the kid's foot with his own, making him look at him. "He would have still adopted you. Mack and my mom? They're not like that. You don't need to worry about that."

"Medicine is always expensive. I don't want to be expensive."

Reece would hug him if he knew him better, and if he didn't also know that fifteen was not a hugging age for boys unless it was with someone you had a thing for. Reece resisted the urge. "Anthony? Don't worry about that. It's not always expensive and, besides, you're part of the family. You came here today for a reason, so you tell me what's going on, we'll get it sorted out."

Anthony nodded, still slouching, still looking uncomfortable. "Jolie caught me testing yesterday. And she's in town today, across the street, but she dropped me off here because she said you would help me. I think it's not in control as much again. I have been getting higher blood-sugar numbers when I check it." He sighed, like every word he managed was another nail in his coffin.

"Listen, I don't know what you've gone through in your life before you came to us, but I want to. Like you said, we're brothers now. Brothers look out for one another. So when I tell you not to worry about this, that the only reaction that Mack and Mom are going to have is concern for you, you can believe me. Jolie didn't lie to you about me helping, and I'm not going to lie to you either." Reece wrote some notes on the chart, giving Anthony some space. "We're going to do a little bloodwork and then get a plan formed, figure out how to get this fully under control. Maybe you've just been doing something different, maybe you could do something different, maybe you need some medicine to help you out. There are a bunch of options, and none of them are a good reason to be upset."

Anthony nodded and sat up a little straighter, rolling up his sleeve, ready for the blood draw. "There might be a reason..."

"What sort of reason?"

"My girlfriend likes to bake..."

Reece laughed. "You think that might be the reason?" A shake of his head and he stood up. "It's not easy to find a girl you like who wants to bake for you. She pretty?"

"She's real pretty,," Anthony confirmed, pulling out his phone and turning it on.

Pretty girl picture, front and center. "Oh, yeah, hard to turn down sweets from her. Give me a second." Reece stepped out long enough to request some supplies, and then sat with Anthony again while they waited. "So the bank is across the street. Is that where Jolie is?"

"She's getting a loan to buy the circus stuff from you for the camp. I can't wait. It's going to be awesome. I'm working out upper body now. Jolie said catchers have to be strong in the upper body."

Catchers. Right, Reece's part of the act they'd been working on before he left. He was going to have to pay a visit to the bank... "I hate to make you wait, but the nurse is going to have to come do the blood draw, and then it will take a few minutes to get the preliminary results. I'm going to step over to the bank and check on Jolie."

"You think she's freaking out?" Anthony asked. "She's been running around all morning, but she gets that look when she goes to town."

Funny that he could be so observant about other people but not confident enough to trust those skills when it came to his place in the family. "I'll just be a couple of minutes..."

CHAPTER SEVEN

JOLIE TREATED ERRANDS like a marathon. In order to get all her business in The World done and over with in one day, she'd happily run herself to the point of exhaustion. Today she'd even kept Anthony home from school and managed to get out in the early morning, get meetings done, get back home to pick Anthony up and drop him at Reece's office, and now she'd check "Bank' off her list. As soon as the loan officer got back from wherever he'd gone to.

She wasn't entirely certain what would happen at the meeting, whether or not he would just discuss options with her or whether he'd have her filling out paperwork. Dealing with banks for the circus and the farm had always been the business of Ginny and Mack. No wonder they'd gravitated to each other. They both had to deal with bureaucracy, and while they might not enjoy it, they were at least competent. Another thing she didn't want Reece to be right about.

He'd said she couldn't go out into the world and get students for the camp. It would be the biggest lie of her life if she tried to say that he was wrong about her not wanting to go out into the world at all. But having him say she couldn't was either a dare or forbidding her to, and both possibilities roused in her the wrong reaction. However ridiculous or immature, shining a spotlight on her weakness made her want to prove him wrong.

But it was more than that. She wanted to prove to herself that she could do this. No matter how good her reasons for wanting to stay safely inside the circus life, those reasons were now a road block that kept her from reaching her next destination.

The door opened and Jolie turned in her seat to look at the man walking in.

"Miss Bohannon, I'm Matt Carmichael. There's a man in the lobby asking for you. He didn't give his name but he said that you would know who he is."

"I know who he is," Jolie said. She didn't need to look and see who it was, but stood and offered a hand to the loan officer in his pigeon-grey suit and overly starched white button-down. "He can wait where he is." She shook his hand and then pointedly closed the door and returned to her seat. Let him watch her, the big jerky know-it-all. "I'm not entirely certain what the meeting is for. I've never applied for any sort of loan before, but with the amount of information about loans and the whole process online, I just wanted to talk to someone face to face. Thank you for agreeing to see me on such short notice."

"You're welcome…"

Before he could continue the door swung open and Reece marched in. "I need to speak with Miss Bohannon for a moment."

"Sir, I really must ask that you wait in the lobby."

"It's okay," Jolie said, sighing and standing. "We'll be quick, Mr. Carmichael. Sorry about this."

He was remarkably okay with the situation, and closed the door behind him when he left.

Reece waited until the man was across the lobby, well out of earshot, before he said, "You're going to get in over your head if you get a loan and try to do everything at once. I know you're angry but everything I said yesterday is still valid. You need to figure out if you have a market before—"

"Do you think this is my first stop of the day?" Jolie kept her voice low, not wanting to get into another shouting match with Reece in public, especially at the place where she hoped to get money to finance the operation Reece was trying to shut down. Him rousing her to make an ass of herself in front of everyone would be a great way to set her up to wreck everything herself.

"I've been to the elementary school, the middle school and the high school this morning. I have phone numbers for different athletics teachers and coaches, I have been to the little dance academy and spoken with the owner about putting up advertising on her bulletin board and whether she'd support having me speak to a couple of her classes to get a feel for things."

She looked out the door, caught Carmichael watching her, and the look he gave asked if she wanted to be rescued. Funny that the suit could be her safety net. A quick shake of her head had Reece turning to look at Carmichael too. His look was much less friendly, she expected.

"You did all that today?"

"Not that I have to justify myself to you, because we both know you're not going to support my decision and you're not going to work with me." Jolie tried to affect a cool tone. She was getting a teensy bit better at dealing with the emotional onslaught, but she could really stand to be totally better at it by now. "Your only purpose here is sabotage. So consider me onto you."

Reece shook his head. "Think whatever you like, I'm trying to protect you."

"I haven't had your protection for the past ten years, and I don't need it now," Jolie reminded him, just in case he'd forgotten she was harboring a grudge and had a damned good reason to do so.

"You just don't want to admit it. If you wanted to claim normalcy, you wouldn't be so stressed about being in public. But have you seen yourself? You only uncross your arms when you have to, and then right back they go. You're trying to do too much too fast."

"Only when you're around," Jolie said, but whether it was true or not she really didn't know. She uncrossed her arms. "Just go. I have a meeting to attend. Though if you want me to think you're on my side, you could tell me what the bid you had for the equipment was. You know, since I should know what I'm getting into financially."

He answered without a second's hesitation. "Just over two million for everything. Both of the big tops, the climate control, the seating, all the sleeper cars the crew live in, the trailers the performers don't own, the actual—"

"So much," Jolie muttered, her astonishment wiping out her anger in a flash. She'd thought she'd been thorough in thinking through the details of starting the camp, in considering the money she'd need… And she had for the rigging and the seats, but the climate control hadn't occurred to her. The sleeper rails weren't necessary for them because this year she only wanted a day camp, but if they went to a sleep-away camp later, there would have to be some kind of facilities for sleeping. Her idea of details and the actual details? Not exactly the same.

He looked smug, and considering how clueless she might actually be, Jolie couldn't blame him for looking smug. But was that all she saw on his features? No. No, he looked greedy too. Two million dollars was a lot of money. "That's the real reason, isn't it? You talk a good game about the difficulty of travelling circuses in this day and age, about the danger to the people you supposedly care about, but at the end of the day you're looking for a fat paycheck."

"Stop it." Reece reached over and grabbed her elbow, giving it a shake. "You know me better than that."

When had she crossed her arms again? "No, I don't. I thought I knew you, but I've had ten years to come to grips with the fact that I never really did. And I'm so stupid... I let flirting, old memories, and *hormones* make me forget that basic truth about you. It's all about Reece. Everything is about you."

Such an idiot. Didn't she ever learn? He may have been Reece when he'd left, but he was Dr. Keightly now.

Reece had to work to keep the frustration from his voice. What did he have to do to make her willing to give him the benefit of the doubt? Even as he asked himself the question, he knew the answer: he had to say yes to the damned camp. So he'd just have to keep dealing with her issues until she gave up, because the camp couldn't happen.

"No matter how badly I behaved in the past, I'm here now. I want to absolve myself by doing what is best by everyone. I'm not your enemy." He let go of her elbow and stepped to the door. Making sure his voice was low, he added, "How many people have been injured in training? More than in the performances. Training is the most dangerous time. When did your shoulder get dislocated? Training, right?"

"No, Reece. Not during training. You don't remember, do you?"

He had been around when it had happened? Reece scoured his memory. She'd fallen a few times, but never to any great harm. "When?"

"Never mind," she muttered, nodding toward the door. "Just go back to work or something."

Through the glass, he could see the suit approaching. He'd said what he'd come to say. She'd either listen or she

wouldn't. Time to go. "We'll talk more about this later."
He stepped out into the lobby.

Jolie called after him in tones anyone who didn't know
her would think were sweet, "Thank you for letting me
know, Dr. Keightly." Reece knew better. That was the Jolie
equivalent of *Screw you, Reece.*

He passed the loan officer, who stepped back into his
office, and for a second he considered throwing Jolie over
his shoulder again and dragging her out of the bank. But
he couldn't do that, not without it affecting his new practice across the street. "Don't sign anything, Jolivetta!"
he yelled instead, even if he knew she probably would.

"Are you all right?" the bank official asked Jolie as he
stepped inside.

Reece stopped and looked back, half expecting Jolie to
say something about how unreasonable he was.

"I'm fine. I'd still like to speak with you about the loan,
though the amount has gone down significantly." The door
swung shut, keeping him from hearing anything else, so
Reece continued out of the bank.

That could have gone much better...

Glad he'd taken a late lunch, Reece came back into Richards's practice, soon to be his practice, and let himself
into the administrative area.

All the gray suddenly bothered him. His head hurt.
Tension headache, and he didn't need medical school to
diagnose that one with how tight his forehead had stayed
bunched since the fight with Jolie.

That had been in color. Not like these gray walls. Pale
gray floor. Darker gray baseboards and furnishings. He
was losing his damned mind—a color bothered him this
much?

Finding the door to Richards's office standing open
and the room empty, Reece walked in and closed the door.

Thank God. He just needed to sit and close his eyes for a few minutes. Close out the monochrome.

More gray. The same thing happened at his apartment, just with a different color. Beige. Beige, beige, beige.

But the farm had color. Green fields and trees. Red and white barns. Pale yellow farmhouses. Blue Keightly logo everywhere.

Red hair. Pink clothes. Jolie.

He had to find some kind of alternative to her camp idea. With the farm being Bohannon property, he couldn't throw her off and tell her to go and find a job.

He could bring her into the office as some kind of office worker maybe. Somewhere he could monitor her, help her if she started to freak out. A couple of hours a week, just to get her used to it.

Except she would be angry with him for even suggesting it. Probably bring Gordy into the office just to prove a point to him. He rubbed at the tension between his brows.

She'd looked nervous at the bank, but most people who were going to talk loans looked nervous. It was just across the street from the practice, he still had some time. He could go back and see how she was handling it. But dropping in once had been enough, considering how that had gone. She might try and beat him to death with a checkbook if he showed up again.

If she was going to go ahead with the camp without him, God only knew how far in over her head she'd get. Not that she wasn't smart, but she had the kind of creative mind that tilted when presented with math and schedules. He was sure she could handle the simple accounting of taking tuition and setting up paychecks for the performers—all she had to do was get the forms on that from his mother—but the overheads would never occur to her. The light bill, water bill, the cost per day for lunches and snacks. Insurance. Inspectors.

He closed the door and dropped onto the couch. The judgy pillow he hated—the one with the eye-searing embroidered flowers and travel advice about the road to hell—rested at the far end of the couch, setting his teeth on edge. He wouldn't let a piece of gaudy fabric change his plans. Taking care of everyone wasn't about having good intentions. It was his responsibility.

The practice was also his responsibility.

When he'd told her he didn't have time, it hadn't been entirely true. He'd considered the amount of time he would be spending to set up a new practice, but the deal with Richards took away a great deal of that. Sure, he had the patients themselves, but he didn't have to worry about all the other stuff it took to set up a brand-new practice. Or deal with the time and money issues that came while establishing a patient base.

He could help her run a camp if he wanted to.

He just wasn't sure he wanted to.

Teaching would be less dangerous for her on a daily basis for her. And with the amount of safety gear available, it could be reasonably safe for the kids. Some things. Not the trapeze though.

A knock on the door roused him from his chair in the dark.

Richards was back. Patients to see.

Time to stop sitting in the dark and do what *he* had been put on this earth for. He couldn't control her any more than he could control Fate. All he could do was try to steer her in the right direction. That would be easier if she trusted him at least a little.

"Dr. Reece Keightly." Reece introduced himself, extending his hand to the first patient in the office the following Wednesday morning. "Dr. Richards is ill today. Have you been informed about my buying the practice, Mrs. Nolan?"

The woman, who looked every ounce the perky soccer mom, shook his hand and smiled. "I have. Nice to meet you. You're one of the circus people, aren't you?"

That had never happened to Reece before he'd decided to settle here. In Nashville, where he'd gone to school, no one had known he was "one of the circus people." "Yes, ma'am. My family have owned Keightly Circus since the early 1800s."

"So you're the one that closed it?"

He hadn't expected that either. "I am." He hooked the stool from below the counter and sat, facing his new patient. "What am I seeing you for today?"

"I actually came because you're here. My daughter Briona? She's thirteen and such a talented gymnast, but two weeks ago her coach told her our Olympic ambitions were a pipe dream. Said that no matter how hard she practices, she's not capable of that level of performance. And she's just crushed. Doesn't want to train any more, even though she loves it. I've just been beside myself, trying to figure out how to help her get through this, and my sister told me there was going to be a circus camp this year on that horse farm outside town. I know how people will be interested, and that space will be limited...but since you're going to be our doctor now, I thought..."

It took him a minute to recover from his surprise. "Actually, it's not certain that there will be a camp yet, Mrs. Nolan. It's not going to be run by the Keightly family, if it even comes to fruition. Jolie Bohannon, whose family traveled with the Keightly Circus for generations, has been researching whether or not it's viable for the area and it's... she's not certain at all that it's going to happen yet." He looked at the chart, noticed that the nurse had taken vitals and left the reason for the visit blank. "So you don't actually need to be seen for anything related to your health?"

"Well, no. Not today. I'm in good health. We're all in

good health, except for how sad my daughter is about her Olympic dream." The Gymnast Mom, not Soccer Mom, smiled at him. "But could you give me contact information for Miss Bohannon? I'd really like to speak with her. Maybe I can help her arrange the camp, if that's part of what is making her hesitate on the decision. I'm a party planner, but I think those same skills could be useful in… It's not going to be an equestrian camp, right? It's a circus camp. Like with juggling and tumbling and maybe trapeze?"

Everyone loved the trapeze. Except him these past ten years.

"You give me your information and I'll pass it to her," Reece cut in, really not having expected this for his first patient flying solo. "And where did you hear about this again?"

"My sister runs the gymnastics studio. That's where Briona, my daughter, got started in gymnastics. Then she moved on pretty quickly when it became clear she could use a private coach. I just want her to have something else to be excited about, and see other possibilities. The performers for circuses are on those TV talent shows, and in Vegas, and all sorts of places. She'd really like—"

Reece waved his hand, smiling at her to hide his irritation. "I'm sure she would enjoy a circus school, but you should know it is dangerous, especially the trapeze. If I were Jolie, I wouldn't offer trapeze at all the first year. That's the major barrier to the camp now, trying to decide how much could be done safely for all children who might want to come, not just those who could be Olympians."

"Oh, I'm sure that can be worked out. Gymnastics is dangerous too, but you just have to try and do it the safest way possible. And I did some research online. There aren't any in the South, but there are a couple of circus schools in New England and on the west coast. And they all look really wonderful."

Nodding, he stood and held out his hand. "I'll pass on your interest, Mrs. Nolan. Just leave your contact information with the receptionist, and I'll move along to the next patient. Wouldn't want to get behind and have Dr. Richards think the new guy can't cut it."

She laughed and stood, shaking his hand longer than he'd actually have liked.

The ghost of Keightly Circus was haunting his practice. Great. He'd thought it was possible that people in the area would put the name association together, but he hadn't expected them to seek him out when this was Jolie's project. It had also never occurred to him to check out what the other circus schools or camps—if there even were any camps—offered.

On Thursday, he was asked about the camp by three more patients.

Friday, his receptionist fielded calls all damned day. They all wanted to know two things. When did it start? How much did it cost?

Richards officially bowed out on Friday. He made himself available by phone in the case of emergency for the following week, but the practice was now Reece's.

He had to talk to Jolie before the practice became her answering service.

"We're going to have a helluva time keeping the kids off the trapeze at night," Granny said, watching the many cousins working to erect the rigging overhead.

"I thought you had them under lock and key when it got dark," Jolie said, kicking back and propping her feet on the raised edge of the ring. Paperwork surrounded her—loan papers, licensing papers, insurance papers, examples of curricula from the few other schools and camps around the country, and an article she'd printed about the ins and outs of starting a summer camp—all stacked in piles of hand-cramping and head-exploding glory.

Choking up the grip on her ink pen, she bent over the clipboard on her lap, writing yet more letters on blank lines and filling in tiny boxes. The paperwork was going to break her.

"The side of the lock that needs a key is on the outside, not the inside," Granny muttered. "And the biggest rascal is Anthony. He's a Bohannon now, and we love him, but that boy has been a little wild since Mack and Ginny went off on their honeymoon."

A tingle at the back of her head had Jolie first lifting her hand to check that a bug wasn't crawling on her neck. No bug. A ponytail pretending to be a rat's nest, half out of the band and tangled, but no bug.

She looked up.

"Reece," Jolie breathed, surprised to see him there.

"No, Reece didn't do anything." Granny shook her head. "But maybe we should have him talk to Anthony. They're brothers now."

"Afternoon, Granny." Reece stepped around the edge of the aisle and walked up, kissing Granny on the cheek. "I'll talk to Anthony. We're getting to know one another, and I'm happy to lend a hand." He looked at all the paperwork and then back at Jolie. "What's all this?"

"Well, I'm gonna leave you two to your damned fight," Granny announced, just before shuffling off. "Got to get dinner on the table, get all these kids fed." Anyone under fifty was a kid to Granny.

"I'll come and help when I get done with Reece," Jolie called after her, her eyes on Reece, who now had his eyes on the rigging installation currently going on. "They're all using safety gear, and always do. Just in case you're worried."

"I'll count on seeing you when you're done. Knowing you two, that should be some time in October…" Granny shook her head and headed away before she really interrupted.

"I'm not worried," he murmured, and then sat down, eyes fixed on the paperwork again, prompting Jolie to answer.

"Loan papers and license papers and other papers." Spreadsheets. Advice from the principals of each school she'd visited. Lots and lots of papers. "We decided that since no one had come to haul off the equipment yet, and no one had told us to take the big top down, we were going to set it all up for inspectors."

"For the camp?" Reece took a seat on the edge of the ring, his voice too calm to be comforting.

"Yes. Everything needs to be inspected before the insurance people can provide good estimates." Was this the kind of calm that preceded an epic eruption? After their big fight the other night, she'd spent about as much time wanting to see him as not wanting to see him. More proof that Reece made her stupid.

"I see. When are the inspectors coming?"

"Tomorrow."

"On a Sunday? Guess I'll be sticking around, then." He picked up a pile of papers and moved them one row down, where more papers awaited her, and took a seat at Jolie's side when a space was made. "I'd like to be here for it."

Heat. The man radiated heat, which made the way the arm nearest him react so weirdly. Goose-bumps rose. Jolie casually wrapped a hand over her arm and rubbed it. Maybe he wouldn't notice. "Why?"

"I have a compromise to offer." He looked down at her arm, but didn't comment.

"I didn't think your expansive doctor vocabulary included that word."

"There you go, doubting my mastery of the English language again." He smiled and Jolie felt herself laughing a little in return.

"Thrill me. Or prove that you don't actually know what that word means. I'm still open to that being the outcome of this conversation, regardless of what you might dub compromise."

"One year. Trial period." He said the words slowly and then put his arm around her shoulders, sliding her the last remaining inches toward him. "Better?"

Definitely better. And worse. "Better how?"

"You're cold."

"Oh." Jolie nodded, mustering a smile in return to cover the lie. She wasn't exactly cold, but her body would probably just love to react more when pressed against his gloriously muscled torso. "Go on, you sound like you have other qualifications."

He nodded, and with the thoughtful way he looked at her, the way he looked at her mouth, she almost lost the thread of the conversation with the urge that came to kiss him. Memories of his mouth on her flesh, of giving her pleasure over to him and the promise he'd kept and those words that still sent chills through her: *I'll never break another promise to you.* She so wanted to believe him.

She moistened her lips, quite willing to throw the paperwork down and kiss him breathless, right there in front of everyone. Dumb. Dumb, dumb, dumb.

"Qualifications," Reece said, clearing his throat, breaking the connection as he looked back up at the rigging being installed. "You're going to be doing most of the work but I want veto power."

He could switch it off. That must mean that most people could switch this kind of thing off. Probably how he'd kept his cool with her and Mr. Happy. Unfortunately, Jolie's emotions still ran wild in his presence. She dug her fingernails into her thigh, a sharp sensation to override the firm heat and heady male scent wrapping around her. Kind of worked. Sort of. She managed to repeat some words back. "Veto power on what?"

"Curriculum. Number of kids you'll take on the first summer. Length of term. And I want all physicals to go through my practice." He unwrapped his arm and scooted a couple inches away, enough room to put his arm between them and gesture upward. "You're setting up the trapeze rigging and net, so you obviously intend on having an aerial component. I want to be the one who does the physicals to determine fitness level for the more advanced—"

Him breaking contact did wonders to clear her head. Terms. She should think about terms. "Wait. So your idea of the compromise is that with your limitations, I get what? To buy the equipment from you? Use the name? What?"

"You have a knot in your hair."

"I know…" she muttered, frowning at his change of direction. Knowing Reece, if she didn't fix it, he'd start trying to get the band out and that would mean touching again. She needed to be able to think. Jolie reached up to start working on the lopsided curly mass. "Go on."

"You get everything. The big tops. The equipment. The mess tent. The safety gear. The name. Costumes. Lady Calliope. Everything."

Everything? Even the calliope? She managed to drag the band from her hair and dragged the locks over her shoulder to begin combing the tangles out with her fingers, and turned so she could see his face better. "Why?" He was hiding something, Jolie just couldn't figure out what.

"For starters, my practice has turned into an answering service for 'When is the circus camp opening?' calls." Reece watched her working on her hair, pensive frown in place, words slow, the fingers of his right hand unconsciously moving, sliding against one another, and she realized he wasn't lying so much as distracted. By her hair. "Second, if you're going to do it, I want a hand in it."

Jolie got most of the auburn riot under control and stopped touching it, returning him the favor of helping clear his mind...in theory. "You said you didn't. You said you didn't want the responsibility." She tossed the lot back over her shoulder, helping more.

He looked back at the installation, allowing her to study his profile. Still thoughtful. "I'll feel responsible no matter what. Even if you go in entirely the opposite direction. Because it is my decision to close Keightly down that made you make alternative plans. But if you use my equipment, at least you can't have too much of a fit if I make demands and set an uncompromising safety standard."

"I never would have had a fit about that, Reece. I'm not sure when you think I turned into a diva..."

"Divas perform. You don't. So you can't be a diva."

"Why does that bother you so much?" Like a dog with a bone...

CHAPTER EIGHT

"Why don't you perform?"

"I told you. I just don't want to any more."

He shook his head, going silent as he watched the Bohannons zip-lining back down to the ground, the last of the rigging in place.

"I figured I wouldn't see you again until the buyers came to take everything away. That's kind of your thing. Show up after being gone, upset plans..."

"I'm not going anywhere." Reece looked fleetingly frustrated, but turned away from her before she could figure out what had caused it. "I told you. The practice is fully mine now—"

"You say that, but you do disappear after every bump? Though this time it's only been a few days. I suppose that's improvement."

"I've been working. You haven't come to my apartment ever, so don't make it sound like I'm the only one who can make the offer."

Okay, so he had a point there. "I guess I didn't know I could. Or I never considered it because when you go, you're gone in my mind." She frowned, feeling a twinge of guilt. "Do you want me to come visit your apartment?"

"Honestly, Jo, I don't know."

Over the past month she'd done more soul searching than she was comfortable with. But recognizing problems didn't mean she knew how to fix them. She'd just started to embrace the idea that maybe she should tell him the realizations. At least then maybe she wouldn't come off as a crazy person. Not everything. She could seem messed up—there probably wasn't any way to avoid that anyhow, but she would like to draw the line before she got certifiable or psycho.

"The whole thing...after the wedding? That freaked you out, right? That's why you don't know whether you want me around, or is it just not wanting to get too tangled up with me? You don't have to say you'll partner with me over the camp as a way to keep anything relationshippy from happening. I told you before, I can take care of my own—"

"No!" he shouted, cutting her off. "Don't say that again." He stood up, rubbing his upper lip in that way that shouted discomfort louder than his shouty voice did. "That's not the reason."

"Fine!" Okay, so she made him feel uncomfortable. That whole business in her trailer had been his idea, or maybe it had been hers? Whatever—it had made him feel uncomfortable. What was she supposed to do with that? Ignore it? That's how she had worked before she'd become the Most Emo Chick in Circusville. She missed that skill, her calm. Her missing serenity...

As he didn't want to talk about it, she put it aside and asked, "Do you want to put the camp stuff in a contract? I know you like to be official and you're putting off a big sale in order to give us a shot at this."

"Not within the company," Reece said. He exhaled roughly, and held out a hand to her. Handshakes still meant something to him at least. Jolie looked at it and then at his face. Business arrangement. Leave all that bad sex and good sex and all the past and everything else out of it. Just focus on the deal and the future, which would be a business arrangement. Not a sexy business arrangement. She'd file all that under "Weddings Make Her Dumber".

She put her hand into his to shake, but she didn't shake it yet. "Say you promise not to sabotage things." And it wasn't underhanded for her to test how serious he was with the promise.

"I don't sabotage things."

She lifted a brow. "Don't even imply that you're direct all the time."

He caught her meaning because he frowned. "Fine. I promise not to sabotage things."

His promises shouldn't mean so much, not with their history, but if he really meant to never break a promise to her... Her heart squeezed and she gave his hand the fastest shake in the world then pulled away to start gathering up her paperwork. "I'll work on getting you figures and if you want to be here for the inspection tomorrow, you will need to just hang out because I don't know exactly when he's arriving. In the afternoon some time. Also, don't forget about talking to Anthony. I think he's got a girlfriend in town. He's on the phone or the computer all hours of the night. Worrying Granny to death. Generally being fifteen."

"You're not happy that I changed my mind?"

"Of course I am. We can do it the right way now, keep the name, and be everything the community would like us to be. Have the iconic tent."

If she looked at him, she'd say the wrong thing. Like admit that whole week after the wedding she'd been thinking about throwing her rules about men out the window and giving him a chance to redeem himself in a full-contact way that involved no toys... And then he'd gone again and she'd decided that he was a massive jerk and she didn't want to do anything with him. But now he was here, and she wanted to again, but not if he was going to keep looking like he couldn't get away from her fast enough.

"I don't believe you."

"That's okay. We're business associates now. It's not your business to see to my happiness. Just a partnership for the camp."

She felt his hand on her chin before she saw him moving closer.

"I'm not shunning you or anything. I'm just trying to be a good guy. Make the right decisions for the right reasons, which usually comes easier to me."

"I don't know what that means." Jolie sighed, wrapping her hand over his in the hope of steering his grip away from her chin.

"Means I'm avoiding certain subjects because that's not coming easily to me with you."

Right. She pushed his hand away, tired of this suddenly. "I don't know what that means either."

Reece leaned down, not letting her get far. The kiss he claimed was slow, hot and full of want. "Means I want you, and I know it's a bad idea. But I'm having a damned hard time caring about whether it's good or bad." He didn't lean back, staying so close that she could feel his lips brush lightly against hers as he spoke, and the scent of his aftershave enveloped her.

"Why is it a bad idea?" Glad she had not yet picked up her sheaf of papers, she let her fingers find his shirt and curl into the material at the waist. "Because you're thinking of running off and becoming a lawyer or something now that you've got the doctor thing done?"

He kissed her again then straightened back up, but kept his arms around her waist, his voice as gentle as if he were talking to a skittish horse. "I'm not the one who's going to be leaving, honey."

"I'm certainly not going to be leaving." Jolie blurted the

words out and then sorted through his implication. "Are you back on that performing thing again?"

"I found you working on an act, but you don't perform. With this camp? You're going to have to. And when this summer is over, you're going to remember how much you love it, and you're going to want to go back on the road with a new circus."

So rational, like a flowchart. She knew doctors would like charts.

"So your big plan to get rid of me is...say yes to the circus camp, so that at the end of a trial season I'll be bored with it. It doesn't matter whether it's a success or not, you think I'm just going to do all this work to build something and then leave because I want to wear Spandex and walk on a wire."

When she put it like that, it did sound kind of like an ass move. Reece shrugged, unfolding his arms so he could rest his hands on her hips, the better to keep her from getting away from him. "I'm not going to lie and say I like it, but I know how miserable you'd be at a desk job."

Jolie reached up and pushed her hair back from her face. "This is not a desk job." A breeze in the nearly empty tent caught at the curls and ruffled them, so they shined like bright copper where the light reflected. He kept his hands on her hips to keep from putting them in her hair.

"You know, maybe you should give me these little snippets of what's going on inside your head more often." Her angry voice alerted him to the depth of the problem. He looked back at her face. "They make me less inclined to think that I'm the problem, because I tend to do that, you know—blame myself. I always think I'm the problem. But when you think I'm a problem, it just makes me mad."

"I don't think you're a problem." Reece hooked a finger in her a belt loop on her jeans as she twirled out of his grasp and dragged her back to him until her back was to his front and he could get his arms around her waist and hold her still. "I think you have a problem. A problem I contributed to when I left. Maybe a problem I caused. If you're missing out on what you want to do because of me... God, Jolie. You need to move on from that. You need to move on from this. Performing is a young business, but you're still young enough to do it. But time won't stand still forever. In ten years..."

"I don't want to move on from this. I don't think this is something bad that needs moving on from. How else can I possibly get that through to you? And how can you continually degrade me for my fear of the outside world, use it as a reason to say no to the camp, and then encourage me to continue the lifestyle that you believe I've just been trying to use to hide from the rest of the world?" She shoved at his forearms and Reece let go, starting to feel a little of her anger himself.

He sat back down, ready to let her get away if she was so determined to flee. "I don't degrade you. I'm just trying to make you think about your future. And you have this huge stumbling block, blinders that don't let you see there is a whole world of opportunity out there for you."

Grabbing the papers, she began stacking them in crisscross fashion, more orderly than he'd have expected from her.

"You can't have it both ways. Either this camp is in the life, or it's not. If it is, why do I need to go anywhere else? If it isn't, why should you want me to go somewhere else?" She shook her head, straightening and looking him dead in the eye, hurt evident in hers. "Everything I need is here. I don't need to go anywhere else."

He was so tired of hurting her. "Why did you build a routine?"

"I'm just playing when I do that." The way she looked down confirmed that she was holding something back.

"You're not being honest with yourself. I want more for you."

"Still. About. You. You don't even see it. They always say that you fall for a man just like your father. Well, call me a cliché. That's exactly what I did."

He was also damned tired of her holding his going away to college over his head. "You have to forgive me for going to school at some point, Jolie."

Movement in the corner of his eye told him they were no longer alone, though he'd thought that everyone had finished with the rigging and left a while ago. But maybe the shouting had drawn someone back.

"I don't need to forgive you for going to school." She walked to the end of the row and down to the ground and back until she was in front of him, if much smaller now from his higher position. "I was upset when you left for a number of reasons. I was afraid something would happen to you out there. That someone would hurt you. That you'd be alone and no one would be there to help you. The fact that I missed you—that I was afraid you would forget me—was secondary. I was terrified *for you*. But I never begrudged you your education."

More tears in her eyes, and the high color on her cheeks matched the high way she held her head. Reece didn't know what to say. Confessing how much he'd missed her would only make her angrier, so he said nothing.

"For the record, I'm proud of what you've accomplished. Everyone here is proud of you for that. Proud enough that I keep forgetting that despite the fact that you want to be the good guy, as you put it, you still cut us out of your life without any warning. You never looked back, and I definitely feel a grudge about that. That was your choice, and you're back here now, wanting to be the good guy? Well, *you'll* have to forgive *me* if I expect you to be the one who leaves. Again. As soon as you can."

"You're right. I did all that. Nothing I can say will change it."

She reached up and swiped her eyes then started walking again. He watched until she rounded the bleachers and walked out of sight.

A couple of seconds later he saw movement again and looked up.

Anthony.

"So, we're brothers now, right?"

Reece nodded. "We're brothers now."

Anthony took the bleachers at a quick climb and sat at a manly distance from him. "I heard you guys fighting. You okay?"

"Not sure what I am. Aside from an ass." And not sure he should be the one getting comforted by the kid who needed a big brother to lean on, not the other way around.

"She was crying." And Anthony had been torn between which one of them to comfort. Reece would probably have chosen to stay away from the weeping woman too.

"I've probably made her cry more than anyone in the world." He leaned his elbows on his knees. "Even her asshole father."

"I don't know which one her dad is. Hard to keep track of them all, just a sea of red hair."

Reece grinned at the teenager, fleeting though it was. It was hard to hold a grin right now. "Her dad wasn't a Bohannon. Her mom is Mack's sister. Seven brothers, one sister that generation. Jolie's dad wasn't born in the life. He tried it, married into the family, but it didn't go very well. Hard on people to suddenly start living on the road."

"So he left?"

"He..." Reece started to explain and then paused, uncertain how much weight his words carried and whether he should share. But Anthony was family now. Thanks to Mom marrying into the Bohannons, there was now an actual link to the Bohannons that went deeper than simply decades of tradition and traveling together. Besides that, everyone knew the story. Not like it was a secret that could ever be kept...so even though he might not want to be the one telling the story, he did want Anthony to open up to him. He should lead by example. "Her dad left when she was five. But he didn't just leave. He took her with him."

"Like kidnapping?"

"Yeah." Reece tried not to picture the broken little girl who'd been brought back home. "Got all the way from Florida to Chicago before he decided he didn't want her. So he gave her a note with contact information for the farm, dumped her in front of a police station, told her to go inside, and left her there so he wouldn't get arrested."

Anthony looked back in the direction Jolie had left. He'd been with the family a couple of years. Jolie's oddities were probably beginning to make a lot of sense to him.

"What happened to her?"

"I don't know exactly. I know they had to fight to get her back. There's an assumption of something negative about the lives of circus families. If not abuse then at the very least dysfunction. I have never asked but, straddling both worlds now, I can speculate about what happened. Social workers, attorneys, questions about why her father stole his child from her mother only to abandon her far away? Very suspicious." Reece shrugged, dismayed at the lack of details he really had about such a big event in her life.

Anthony looked around the tent, and Reece couldn't read past the scowl the young man wore. Either he was just angry or he was really trying to work through what

Reece had told him. "But wouldn't she have to look abused for them to think that?"

"She was a wild little thing before. Fearless. And clumsy. I've never seen a picture of her where she didn't have some kind of bruises or scrapes. Put it with the other questions…and they put her into a group home for a week or something, until it was sorted out. By the time we got her back…she was different."

Terrified all the time. Wouldn't let go of his hand, even when she'd had to go to the bathroom. Reece could remember standing with one arm in the bathroom stall and the rest of his body outside the door, giving her the most privacy he could because she wouldn't even let go of his hand to go to the bathroom. Just the one good hand, the other had been in that pink sling.

Oh, hell. That had been for her shoulder…not her arm.

"And then you left her too," Anthony filled in, pulling Reece's attention back with a simple statement that ate through his gut.

Reece nodded. And she'd been afraid someone would hurt him. He really was an asshole.

Anthony shook off the scowl on his face, leaned forward to punch Reece in the leg. "Tell her you're sorry, man."

"It's not that simple." Such a good-natured kid. Impossible not to like him. And if Reece ever doubted how much he'd missed his family, being presented with a kid brother intent on taking care of *him*…there was just no way he was leaving again.

"Sure it is. You're sorry." Anthony mustered a smile, shrugging. "Whatever reasons you had for what you did don't matter. You're sorry. Tell her. That's why she talks so much."

"What do you mean?"

"I don't know Jolie real well, but I watch people. She

talks when she's confused, trying to work stuff out." He tapped the side of his head. "And she used to be a lot quieter. Actually, she used to be a lot calmer too. She's been riled up since you got back."

"You watch people, eh?"

"I'm going to be a writer, I pay attention."

"What are you going to write?" Reece asked.

"Deep stuff; it'll blow your mind."

Reece laughed finally and stood up. "I don't doubt it." Presented with a fist, Reece bumped his against it and tilted his head. "Granny won't save dinner if you're not there."

"She'll save food for me. I'm her favorite."

And Reece's favorite too, but he cupped the back of the kid's neck and gave him a light shove toward the exit. "Fine, she won't save me any. And if I'm going to talk to Jolie again, I'd better fortify myself."

And he was supposed to talk to the kid about…something. "Don't stay up so late on the phone with your girl-friend. You might be Granny's favorite, but she'll still chew you up in the foulest language you ever heard if you don't do what she says."

"I mind."

"Two words, man: Manure duty."

A sexy blues instrumental didn't go with the horrific bu-reaucratic forms in Jolie's lap. But what really could go with this kind of insanity? Funeral-home music maybe.

She switched to a new stack of papers, just for something else to look at. Tuition schedules. She'd based them on the idea of paying back loans. Now she wasn't sure how to do it—just change the destination of the monthly payment to Reece as a wage? It was his equipment, and even if he was going to endow the farm with the money, he should be the one to actually do with it what he would.

Talking to him was unavoidable.

Jolie didn't know what was worse—trying to make it through a single conversation with him without being overwhelmed by some emotion or another, or the hours of introspection afterwards when she relived—

A loud knock on the door rattled her trailer, startling her. She yelped and the very next second Reece had the door open and was standing on her entrance stairs.

"You cried out."

"You almost banged a hole in the door."

He came more fully inside, closed the door and stepped around her piles of paper to sit on the couch.

"Oh, come on in, Reece. Sure. Have a seat. Pay no attention..." Now where was she going to run away to? Maybe she should start talking about all the men she was going to sleep with now that he'd made Mr. Happy seem like Mr. Crappy, Lame and Boring...

"If I'd asked, you might have said no. And I'm here to apologize."

Apologize? She slowly lowered the pages to peer at him over the edge. "For what?"

"Everything."

"Everything?" Well, that cleared it right up.

He nodded, looking her in the eye and then shrugging. "I'm sorry."

Her stomach twisted and she crawled over the papers and onto the couch beside him, turned sideways to face him but stayed far enough away to avoid touching him. "Care to expand on what 'everything' means?"

"For hurting you."

"For not calling? Not writing? For disappearing for ten years?"

He kept eye contact, but the wince told her his apology didn't extend that far. "I had to cut off all contact with you."

Either he just didn't get it or he was trying to get out of actually admitting what had happened...and maybe what had driven him to it. "Why?"

"Because...I just had to." Definitely didn't want to admit anything.

"Were you in the witness protection program?"

He made another face. "No."

"A coma?"

"Jo..."

"Did you get abducted by aliens?"

"Jolie..."

"I know, you were a secret agent and—"

"You've made your point."

She shook her head. "Your turn."

"Nothing I can say will give you any kind of peace. But that doesn't mean I'm not sorry. I want to make things right with you."

"You can't make things right with me without an explanation. If you just want to say you're sorry and have me forgive you...okay. I will stop bringing it up. I won't ask any more. I'll forgive you, and I'll try to forget. Maybe we can even be friends someday... But you can't make it right without telling me the truth. You can't leave this big hole and make it right, even if what you have to say hurts. I deserve an explanation."

"I would have quit school and come back the instant you asked me to," Reece muttered. "I didn't know any other way to stay in school than to just...try to forget you."

The words hurt, but they really shouldn't surprise her. She needed to hear them, she just couldn't look at him while he said them. "Did it work?"

"No."

That was something. Jolie slumped back against the arm of the couch as she listened, her hand going to the fringe of the throw draped across the back, something to play with, something to focus on, something to keep her calm as she listened.

"It wasn't my plan when I left. But before we even got to the campus...I knew I couldn't come back. If I didn't stay away, nothing would ever change. And then someone else would die because that's the nature of the business. And maybe some death would happen that I could have prevented if I'd stuck to my convictions...and I'd have borne more responsibility because I didn't know how to make everyone listen to me. Keightly became my responsibility the instant my father died, and he taught me to protect. But I was nineteen. I couldn't protect anyone."

The truth rang in his voice and reflected in the sadness in his eyes, and she knew how his father's death had hit him. She'd seen him change but hadn't known how to help him. It was the truth to him. He couldn't know she wouldn't have asked him to give up his schooling.

"What are you thinking?"

What was she thinking? "I don't know. Wishing I'd known, I guess. It took me a long time to give up on you." She abandoned the fringe and swiped her cheeks when she realized she'd started crying again. "By the time I accepted that you weren't coming back...I think I was numb. It didn't hurt that much then. I was calm. And I've been having a hard time getting my calm back since you got here. Really would like to get that back. When I'm happy, I'm happier. When I'm sad, I'm sadder. Like...everything is catching up. It's too much. I hate it." Of course her tissues were all the way on the other side of him. She took a wobbly breath and then crawled forward, leaning over him to cram her hand into the tissue box. "And now I'm out of tissues!"

Which just made her want to cry more.

"Stay here." He stopped her before she could lean back,

turned her and when she sat across his thighs he wrapped his arms around her.

"I'm sorry. I keep crying, and I don't mean to. Is this a panic attack too?" She pressed her eyes against the side of his neck, her face hot all over.

"You don't have to be sorry." Reece stretched out as much as he could on the sofa, keeping her on top of him, her face hidden in his neck. His voice was gentle. "I think this is something else."

"I'm crazy."

"You're not crazy. Just let it happen. I'm not going anywhere."

More breaking rule number two. Too overwhelmed to fight it, she relaxed against him and cried long past the point when she even knew what she was crying about, but he never wavered. Never tried to get out from under her.

"Your shirt's all wet." She lifted her head and looked at him. "Do you still want to be in business with a crazy chick?"

"You think this is news? I knew you were nuts the minute I saw your crazy hair. But do you feel better?"

She nodded and he kneaded the back of her head and tugged her forward to press his lips to her forehead.

"I forgive you even if you're an idiot."

He tilted his head until it was his forehead against hers. "Thank you."

"I'm going to get off you before I attack you. I do have one grudge left, but I think we've probably dug deep enough for one night, don't you?"

"What is it?"

She climbed off, fetched a paper towel from the kitchen and blew her nose. "You made Mr. Happy seem very lame."

He laughed as he rolled to his feet. "I'm trying very

hard not to ever say those words, turn them into innuendo, or hit on you…"

"The runny nose is a real turn-off." She blew her nose again. "And the red puffy eyes."

"Not so much." He tilted his head toward the bedroom. "I could sleep, though. If you didn't mind me staying. I'd really like…"

"So you can be here for the inspectors?"

"No. I could stay at the RV and be here for the inspectors." He looked her in the eye and smiled. "You want more confessions? Okay, I just want to stay. You got up before I got done holding onto you."

A nod was all she could pull off. Sometimes words meant too much. A nod didn't amount to promises. When morning came, she reminded herself, everything might look different.

No promises tonight. She didn't want him to fail any tests right now.

CHAPTER NINE

HEAT AT HER back and all around her, Jolie shifted in the bed, aware first of the heat and then the source of it. Reece, at her back, warm breath in her hair.

She grabbed the blanket that was over both of them and tossed it back behind him, as smoothly as she could to avoid waking him, leaving them both covered only in a sheet. She wanted a few minutes to enjoy his presence before things got hard again. They always seemed to get hard again when they each had so many issues bubbling beneath the surface.

The early morning sun hit the windows above their heads, making the pale yellow curtains glow gold. She shifted around in his arms, suddenly struck by an intense need to look at him.

His shoulder-length hair, always tied back from his face, was loose and a sandy lock draped across his forehead. Golden eyelashes fanned his cheeks, hiding those blue eyes she loved.

Carefully, she linked her fingers with his and scooted in until her forehead rested against the two days of beard scruff on his neck. His scent mingled with hers, and her bed became a strange and wonderful place. Full and safe.

She wanted this. She wanted him. For however long it lasted. If she prepared herself for the end before they got started, maybe it wouldn't be so bad when he left. He might stay until the end of the summer, seeing as that's when he was sure she was going to leave. Facing up to the fact that he was wrong might make him leave again.

That wasn't what she needed to think about this morning, it would only lead to dark places, and she had a warm, glowing bedroom and a golden man holding her. Not the time for dark places.

Jolie tilted her head and pressed her lips to his neck—a couple of slow, lingering kisses to encourage him to wake.

He smiled. She didn't see it, but she felt his jaw move against her temple and she leaned up to look at him.

"Morning," he said, stretching until his feet hung over the bottom edge of her bed.

Jolie grinned back and kissed his chin, then his cheek.

When he'd got that pesky stretching out of the way, Reece grabbed her and rolled onto his back so she rested atop him again. Her legs fell to either side of his hips, but that was all the rearranging she had time for. His hands moved to her hair and tugged her head down until their lips met. His tongue stroked hers and his arousal roared to life between her legs, but the cotton pajama shorts she slept in and his boxers kept any accidents at bay. Which meant she could practice moving against him, find out what made him moan.

The last time he'd been in her bed he'd turned her beliefs upside down and had taken no relief for himself. Now she wanted to see that kind of need in his eyes, to make him tremble and shake.

She wanted some kind of reassurance that she could be good enough for him. If he wanted her half as badly as she wanted him, that would be good enough for most people. It was a good starting place...

She knew how to move, the long sinuous rolls of her spine and her hips, until she rode the ridge of his erection through the cloth.

"Jo…" He groaned her name against her lips. "I don't have condoms."

She pulled back, and he relaxed his hold on her hair to let her, but only until she could look him in the eye. She smiled. "I got some the day after we played with Mr. Happy."

"Oh, thank God."

The relief in his voice made her smile. "I would have thought…"

"I've been trying to be the good guy."

"The good guy gets condoms."

"Temptation." He shook his head then rolled them again until she was beneath him. He rose to his knees, suddenly very interested in getting her clothes off.

No slow seduction.

Good. His need gave her confidence.

He dragged her shorts and panties down with one go. Jolie tugged the shirt over her head then reached for his boxers. "I'm tempted to make you stand up so I can properly see wha—"

His boxers were already down and her words died in her throat. "Good God, I'm throwing away Mr. Happy."

This time he laughed, then leaned into her again, pulling her legs around his hips as he claimed her mouth once more.

Reece lifted up enough to give himself a grand view of her beneath him. Her auburn curls spread across the yellow pillowcase, her milky skin and freckles, and the palest, pinkest, most pert…

"I want to be on top," Jolie panted, pulling his gaze back to her rapidly pinkening face.

"You haven't really done this before." No. Don't refer to the other time.

Her brows pinched and she reached up, rubbing her

hands over his chest, making him inclined to do whatever she wanted. Because nothing had ever felt more right and it wasn't rocket science.

His inner caveman screamed that she'd been given to him. His father had given her to him to take care of. She was his. Always had been his. Always would be his. Jolie, his Jolie. He kissed her again.

"I was doing it right when we were clothed...wasn't I?" The question rumbled against his lips between kisses.

She wanted to be in control, which might be another test. And she might need reassurance. "You were perfect."

She'd accused him of being a control freak a couple of times, and then there was the method of their last tryst when he'd controlled the toy... It would be great if he could just act, stop second-guessing, but she was wrong—he wasn't a control freak. Reece grabbed her hips and rolled again. "Okay, if you change your mind..."

"I won't." She sat up and the gloriously slick heat ground against him. Every ounce of him wanted to flip her back over, take her, drive himself into her until she knew she belonged to him. Until he got his reason back. Until that hold she had over him was at least a little weaker...

But he'd always need to protect her. "Where are the condoms?"

She leaned to the side, fished around in the drawer, grabbed her toy and tossed it across the room, then found what she was looking for.

And if she wanted control of the condom, it would have to wait for next time. Reece plucked it from her fingers, tore the foil and slid her down his thighs until he got the thing on.

Sitting up, he grabbed her and dragged her back to him, unable to abide all that air between them. He eased into her. All he had to do was last longer than a few seconds and he'd do better than the other time...but he wanted her shaking and moaning for him, not that damned toy.

After a few tentative, experimental shifts and grinds against him, she found a natural rhythm that made him sweat. Reece grabbed her hips, trying to hold onto some semblance of control. If he didn't...he'd disappoint her again.

"Don't... You liked it," Jolie gasped as he slowed her down. "I want you to like it...a lot."

"I do." He gritted his teeth, tugging her back down with him as he lay back in the bed.

Kissing could always distract her, and he thrust his tongue into her mouth, hands tangling in her hair again. Every rock of her hips got him a little closer to a poor showing. She deserved the best, this was practically her first time as he'd ruined the actual first time.

When he felt his orgasm building at a speed that left him in little doubt that if she kept moving another few seconds he'd be lost, Reece gave in to his need for her orgasm and flipped them again, pulling out before he got there.

The hurt look on her face knocked the wind out of him. "Why? Why did you do that?"

"Jo. I need to... I need... I need to make you come."

Jolie felt him shaking where he knelt between her legs. That and the tortured light in his eyes soothed her. This wasn't because he didn't want her. It was his control issues. Even telling her he needed anything was kind of a milestone.

She nodded, and he crawled back over her, his kiss gentling this time as he began a sensual onslaught that wiped out her ability to worry.

Only golden light today. No dark places.

* * *

Once all the details had been finalized and the nightmare days of form-filling were past, completing the actual physical needs for starting the camp were a breeze. If you counted out the conversation both Jolie and Reece were avoiding. An impending showdown over the trapeze.

First day today, and Reece was going to come for the day, but he hadn't stayed with her last night. The first night in the past couple weeks he hadn't. It had taken a while to get to the bedroom, but once they had, neither had been eager to leave it.

It was better for both of them and their fledgling relationship to try and work together in things.

He'd needed an evening to himself and she'd given it to him.

She needed to be reassured regularly that he wasn't going anywhere, and he gave that to her. Any time she got nervous, so, like…every day.

Reece needed to run the physicals for the kids with exacting demands and limits, and she knew why he needed it…so it was no hardship for her to help. Over two weekends leading up to the opening they'd held an open clinic for the campers and he'd put them through the wringer. Health checks. Endurance trials. Games designed to test speed and reaction times. A little over the top for the kids who were going to be working with choreography, costume and set design…but she hung in there.

Jolie finished getting dressed for opening day in a T-shirt identifying her as an instructor and the equipment she'd need for her tightrope class. Along with a few other miscellaneous bits and pieces she'd need for demonstrations with the older instructors and their classes.

During the past two weeks Reece had also started working with Anthony on the monkey bars, starting slowly with the basics of how to be a catcher—a position they both hoped Reece could eventually hand off to Anthony. He decidedly did not want to get on the trapeze. Jolie didn't think he was afraid so much as he had developed an intense loathing for flying after his father had died. And that was the talk they had been avoiding.

When they'd been working to get her into his family's troupe in their teens, it had taken Reece three months to learn to just catch her with any kind of consistency. Three months of leaping and falling before they'd found the rhythm, learned to time their swings and he could catch her eight times of ten. And when they'd begun throwing tricks, it had taken another several months before each one was better than it was worse.

Anthony would not be ready to catch until maybe the end of the season. Having him in the show planned for the end was a possibility, but the other aerialists needed to practice their tricks with someone who could catch them the rest of the time. She had to have that talk with Reece.

Later.

After no one died on their first day.

With breakfast done, and a full hour before the kids were due to start arriving, Jolie wandered into the big top and found Reece alone on a zip-line, hanging from the canopy as he inspected the rigging. Again. She really shouldn't be surprised by now. This was the third time she'd caught him inspecting the equipment. A socket wrench in hand, he methodically made his way around every part of the connection before him, and then carefully maneuvered himself further down.

Safety Man did not like risks of any kind. And while this was something Jolie could appreciate, she did not want him up there when the parents and kids started arriving. She grabbed one of the megaphones and—once he'd anchored himself again—lifted it to her mouth. "Reece

Keightly, you had an inspector here. And now you're quadruple-checking to make sure it's good?"

He shot a thumbs-up at her.

"Twenty minutes and I'm coming up after you. You promised— no sabotaging the camp! Scaring the parents counts as sabotage."

"Almost done!" he bellowed back down.

Jolie sighed, put the bellowing apparatus down, and headed toward her class area. Most of the seating had been cleared out of the big top to make more room for the different classes to work in the tent at once. Having been a one-ring circus meant that they'd never shared space before.

Kicking off her shoes, she put on the soft-soled leather slippers Angela had made for her ages ago, and which the costuming maven had duplicated for her five students from impressions made during registration.

She limbered up and climbed onto the low wire with the rodless umbrella in hand she preferred for balance. And by the time she'd run the length of the wire a few times, Reece came strolling toward her.

Not knowing any other way to approach the question on her mind, she blurted it out. "Anthony isn't going to be ready to catch when they are ready to start learning to fly."

"I know." He watched her. "Do that little hopping thing. Where you change your feet. What's that called?"

"I don't know terms. It's a ballet thing, but I couldn't keep the language in my head. I tried. Just…didn't work." And it looked more impressive than it actually was, one of the easier things she did. She gave the little hop he'd requested, back and forth a few times, and found him smiling at her when she stopped and took the second needed to restore her balance. "Good to see you smiling. Happens so infrequently in the tent."

He stepped over and took her free hand, and she made the little hop onto the mats. "Are you ready for this?"

"I'm excited. But we still need to talk about the trapeze."

"We don't need to talk about it. I know what I have to do. I promised to be a good...whatever I am, and I will do what is needed. But the sooner I can get Anthony up and running on it..."

She leaned up, wrapping an arm around his neck and urging him down. "Kiss me. Make it count because we can't be kissing when the kids are here." And they still had a few minutes before the Big Excitement began for her, and the Big Scary began for him.

Having made a promise to never break a promise to her gave Jolie a great big stick to hold over Reece's head. Especially as he'd also promised not to sabotage the camp. Had given his stamp of approval on the squad selected for the aerial act. And now he had to do what he absolutely did not want to do. Get on the trapeze.

He looked at a sea of faces, all forty children cleared to attend, that wanted to see the trapeze demonstration. The ones selected for the aerial troupe had been practicing swinging out and letting go of the bar all week, since the opening, safety lines controlling their falls to the net. Reece was supposed to catch Jolie, that's what they hadn't seen. That's what he'd be doing for them until Anthony was ready. Which, naturally, meant he had even more responsibility on his shoulders should one of them get hurt.

While Jolie talked to the kids, explaining what he did to all the non-aerialists who'd just stayed late with their parents to watch, he hooked himself to the safety harness. He hadn't used one to climb the ladder since he'd started flying at eight, but teaching them the safest way possible was important. He hooked into the lines and climbed rapidly to the platform above. Practice swings at ground level had been set up for them to practice hanging, mats beneath and spotters. He'd even used one to make his body remember what the hell it was doing, but he needed a few minutes above ground to get used to everything again.

Just like riding a bike, and possibly just like falling off one.

He unhooked the safety lines and the swing, tuned out whatever was going on with the audience below and stepped off the platform.

Suspended from the bar by his hands, he pulled into the swing. It had been easier to achieve the biggest swing when he'd been fifty pounds lighter.

All he heard was the blood pounding in his ears. Jolie might not get dizzy any more, but he'd been grounded a while. It took effort to remember how to do everything he was supposed to do.

At the height of his swing—as high as he was willing to push it for demonstration—he flipped himself and hooked his legs on the bar. He was the catcher. He wouldn't be doing tricks, he wouldn't be dropping, unless it would hold two hundred but not three when he caught Jolie…and they fell into the net and he crushed her to death. Would blood look the same in sand as it had in the sawdust?

Closing his eyes, he let the swing take him.

It wasn't going to get better. He could do it, but the thrill was well and truly gone.

Reece opened his eyes, pulled up on the swing to a sitting position and gave Jolie the thumbs-up.

She repeated his procedure, wrapping a belt around her middle and hooking safety lines before she climbed to the platform. But she switched things up when she also hooked her megaphone to the belt and carried it aloft.

"So what we're going to do…" She began explaining the mechanics of a simple hand-off. Both hanging by their knees, clasping hands in the middle, and her letting go. The first thing Reece was willing to teach the kids.

He waited on the swing, which now only swung a little. He'd have to work to get it going again when the time came. She talked longer than he'd expected, long enough that the kids were getting antsy before she put the megaphone down and looked at him.

"Scared?" he mouthed at her, standing on the swing but not starting the swing until he was sure she wanted to do this.

She shook her head, unhooked the swing and held it with one hand while holding onto the platform supports with the other. "Ready."

Her pale face said she was lying. Right. Something to make her promise later...to tell him the damned truth even when she didn't want to admit to something. He frowned and looked down at the small audience. If it were anything but a knee hang, he'd call it off. But they were about the safest thing that could be done on the trapeze.

Soon his swing was at height and he lowered himself back to the bar. When he reached the right distance from his platform, he yelled, "Hep!" And she took off. When they met in the middle, she turned over to hook her knees on the bar. When he reached the platform, he did the same.

When they met in the middle again, he caught her wrists, she released the bar, and they swung free. She smiled, but there was no ease in her grin and none of the light that he had always seen when she performed. She really was struggling. "Okay?" he asked, and she nodded. They wouldn't get to talk again until he had caught her.

"Rusty," she assured him and then nodded. "Let go."

Reece hated this part. When they got to the middle, he had to force his hands to unlock and she fell to the net. Normally there would be a partner on the platform to swing out to her again, enabling her return to the platform, but they were a two-person show today. He stayed upside down, watching as she flattened out and bounced a couple of times in the center of the net.

Perfect. Safe. Everything was okay. He rose back up to a sitting position, letting the blood drain back out of his throbbing head.

She exited the net as she'd taught the children, hooked back into the safety and climbed back toward the platform. But by the time she got there she was a little rosier in the cheek. Enough to convince him that she was okay to go again.

As Reece stood and got the swing going again, she explained what they were going to do with the megaphone. And then she explained some more. At least three times she started to put the megaphone down, only to stop and add something unnecessary to her explanation. The third time she put it down she very nearly reached for it again, but changed her mind and reached for the swing hook instead, which she used to retrieve her swing.

They were definitely having a talk when this was over.

By the time she got the swing back, the hook stashed, and had given the lying nod that said she was ready, Reece had his swing high enough. At the height of the swing he slid back to the bar and on his mark called for her to go.

One each, swinging forward and back, and by the time they met in the middle, they were synchronized to catch the trick.

Reece reached, and Jolie let go of the bar, but she didn't reach for him until she'd already fallen out of his reach. His hands closed on air, his stomach lurched, and he watched her flatten and fall onto the net.

He pulled himself back above the bar before he threw up, and watched her exit the net and stop to say something to the kids before she repeated her procedure to get back up to the platform and get ready. She didn't look at him, just announced she was ready and waited.

Reece didn't start swinging until she looked at him.

"What's wrong?" No mouthing anything now, he yelled across to her, regardless of whether or not everyone would hear. This was her camp, she was the one who had insisted on an aerial component, and she had blown that catch.

"Nothing. Just rusty," she yelled back, scowling at him and adding a quick jerk of her head intended to get him moving again.

Reece took a couple of deep breaths, stood, and started the swing going again.

Once more she released the bar and Reece's hands made contact with her arms this time, sliding all the way down to the wrists, where they should lock, but before he could complete the action she jerked her arms free and fell once more to the net.

She'd rather fall than have him catch her?

Reece pulled back up and watched her bounce and then move off the net and march for the other end again. Not again. No.

Before she could get herself secured and climb, Reece swung to the middle of the net and hopped off the bar, letting himself fall into the net below.

He got down and headed for the kids. "Sorry, guys. We're done for the evening. Jolie's getting over a vertigo thing. She thought she was ready, and she wanted to do this for you guys, but her inner ear isn't co-operating." When he got many confused looks in return, he pointed to his ear and explained, "Squiggly bits deep inside your ear that control balance. We'll see you all Monday and the trick will be demonstrated before any of the kids go up on the bar."

Everyone was very understanding of that, except Jolie, who stood out of the way, yanking on the hand guards she wore to try and unbuckle the straps that held them in place. He left the group and walked up to her, his nausea almost a memory now that his feet were on the ground.

"What was that?" He took one of her hands and unfastened the buckles giving her fits.

"I don't know."

"You always say that when you don't want to admit something." He pulled the guard off and held his hand out for her other hand, which she placed in his. "So you can reach your hand into mine. Just maybe not when there's danger involved? Did you think I'd fling you off the net or something?"

CHAPTER TEN

JOLIE SHOOK HER HEAD. "I really don't know what happened."

"All you had to do was close your hands around my wrists." The guard came off in his hands, and she tried to pull her hand back, but his hand clamped down and held her in place.

"I know." Why hadn't she grabbed onto him? They were together now. In a relationship. Having mind-blowing sex, working together...practically living together, and she couldn't make herself reach for him. "I'm sorry."

Reece shook his head, and she noticed that he was pale. "Are you sick?"

"Yes. Yes, Jo. Not catching you? I almost hurled on your head. Twice. You did fine on the knee-hang. I don't get it."

"I don't know. I don't get it either."

"You need to think about it."

"I don't want to."

"Yes, I know, that is how you got through the past ten years, but you have to stop ignoring problems. If we're going to be together, if we're going to try and make this work, as we said we were going to, you have to find some way to trust me."

"I do trust you."

"No, honey, you don't trust me. If you trusted me, you

wouldn't have ripped your arms from my grasp and let yourself fall, instead of relying on me."

Jolie sucked in a breath. She wanted to argue with him, but what good would that do? She'd said she'd forgiven him, and she had...but maybe it would never matter how many promises he kept. Maybe she was too messed up to trust anyone.

"Is it me, or is it everyone?"

She looked up at his quietly spoken question and then stepped in to wrap her arms around his waist. "What do you mean?"

"Do you just not trust me, or do you not trust anyone?"

"I trust you. I do. You've been great. You didn't want to catch but you tried. And I know you've been working with Anthony since he wants to catch for the end of season show. You've been great." She laid her forehead against the center of his chest and mumbled, "I'm reaching now. See?" She shook her arms around his waist. He gave in to the hint and wrapped his arms around her.

"No camp stuff tomorrow. We're going out."

"I have things—"

"Hey..." He waited for her to look up at him and said, "You can do them on Sunday. Tomorrow we're going out."

"Like riding?"

"No. Like out into the world. Date. We're going out, you and me. Not on errands. Not to get groceries or go to the bank. We're going out. Dress casual, wear comfortable walking shoes." He leaned down and kissed her and, as always, she melted into him and her anxiety started to do the same. Before she could get lost in it, he lifted his head and put her back from him. "I'll pick you up at ten. Wear one of your camp shirts."

"You're not staying with me?"

"Not tonight."

He was mad. Which...she couldn't blame him for.

"Ten," he said again, then turned and headed out, leaving her to stare at the trapeze and, eventually, to clean up and shut everything down.

Going out into the world to spend time? Definitely a punishment for not reaching for him.

At least she didn't have to wear heels for it.

"Where are we going?"

Reece looked over at Jolie. That had been the third time she'd asked since he'd wrangled her into his SUV forty minutes ago.

"You say you trust me, but you can't take it that I won't tell you. It's a surprise." Reece shook his head. "If you were paying attention to the highway signs, instead of just sulking and staring at the blur, you'd have figured it out by now." Yesterday had been one of his buttons, but he'd got on the trapeze for her. She could go on a date with him in a public place for him.

"I don't like surprises. And I'm not sulking. I'm listing the reasons that everything is going to be okay." She crossed her arms and frowned but sat up a little straighter and focused immediately on the massive approaching sign. "The zoo?"

"The zoo."

"There will be a lot of people there."

"That's why I wanted you to wear your camp shirt." He looked at the matching Keightly Circus Camp T-shirt he was wearing. "So this is like a business outing too. Good for the camp. Lots of people will be here with their kids, and Keightly has been in the news a lot lately with the circus closing and now with the camp up and running. Have you been here before?"

"No," Jolie admitted, climbing out of the car and pausing to adjust everything, including the hang of her T-shirt so that it looked perfect.

When he offered his hand to her, she had to stop and wipe her hands on her shorts before she took it. Sweaty palms. But no panic attack yet. With the new information she'd given him about her out-of-control emotions since his return, he didn't know whether to expect another panic attack or not. Whether her anxiety at being out in the world would be increased in his presence or decreased, he had no idea.

"It'll be okay." He closed his hand around hers, and then thought better of it and linked their fingers. More secure hold. Maybe the little things would help her. "And you're going to like the zoo. Lots of animals... And we're going to go straight to the kids' area. I don't know what it's called. There's a petting zoo and other things there. So lots of kids. Lots of animals. You can pet a camel or... something else that doesn't bite."

Petting zoos, an idea Reece could get behind. They weeded out the dangerous animals.

She nodded but looked less convinced than he was, and stayed close as he walked them through the ticket booth to the park. Maybe his presence did help her.

It would be great if he could find some simple way to fix his problem with the trapeze.

For the first hour of their visit Jolie stuck to Reece like glue. They wandered through the petting zoo, they ventured out to the see the monkeys, and when she wanted to go back to the child area, he didn't put up a fuss or make her feel bad about it.

Camels, llamas and sheep, and Jolie liked the sheep best. Domesticated animals trumped exotic ones. They could be trained and didn't often eat their owners. But watching the kids with the animals was the best of all. Their glee was an easy emotion for her to identify with and wrap herself in.

And when her eyes skimmed over a little boy of about

five, wandering alone with tears in his eyes, she knew that emotion too. Releasing Reece's hand for the first time since they'd arrived, she walked over to the little boy and touched his shoulder. "Are you looking for your mom?"

As soon as she asked the question he started to cry. Most kids outgrew her by the sixth grade, but she was still taller than a five-year-old, and if she'd learned anything from Reece and their fights it was the importance of minimizing your height when someone was already scared or upset.

She squatted, keeping eye contact, and spoke in her gentlest voice. Soon she had his name, the identity of who he'd been with, and at least a small measure of his confidence. She'd always liked kids. "Don't worry, Drew. We'll find your daddy."

He nodded, swiping his eyes with the back of his hand.

"Do you remember what color shirt your daddy was wearing?"

She felt Reece approaching, and the little boy suddenly taking her hand confirmed it. "It's okay. That's Reece. He's my friend. He'll help us find your dad. What color is his shirt?" she asked again, giving the boy's hand a jiggle until he connected with her gaze again.

"White."

Great. A man in a white shirt. That wouldn't help.

"Don't be scared. Everything is going to be okay." She looked around, but seeing over the crowd was as hopeless for her as it was for the little boy. And Reece didn't know who he was looking for any more than she did.

Surely no one would abandon their kid at a zoo. That wouldn't happen. Who would pay the ticket price and walk through cameras and be on security footage when they abandoned their kid? No one. People who abandoned their children worked to retain anonymity. "He's got to be looking too. Do you see anyone looking?" she asked Reece.

Reece glanced around but shook his head and asked Drew, who still held Jolie's hand, "What's your dad's name?"

"Will you put him on your shoulders?" Jolie redirected.

"My shoulders?"

It took a dose of convincing for both Reece and Drew to agree to the maneuver, but soon Reece had Drew on his shoulders and standing. It took less than a minute before the worried father cut through the crowd and relieved Reece of his tow-headed shoulder-growth. After many thanks, Reece steered her to the cotton-candy stand and got her a fluffy pink treat.

A shaded bench nearby? Even better. She hurried to it and sat, then offered a pinch of the wispy spun sugar to Reece.

"You told me that I have to think about...emotions and things?"

"I asked you to think about them," Reece corrected, but popped the candy into his mouth.

She ignored the semantics and forced herself to look Reece in the eye. "That's what I feel like when I'm...in big public places like this."

"Like Drew?"

"Like I'm lost...or like whoever I'm with will leave me there and I'll be by myself and I won't know what to do. Which sounds really stupid now that I say it out loud."

"Jolie, you had that happen. Well, you had worse. It's not stupid. It's wrong, but it's not stupid." He took another pinch of the cotton candy and held it to her mouth. She took it and while the fruity fuzz dissolved on her tongue he added, "You knew what to do to help Drew. Some outside-the-box thinking but it got the job done. I would probably have just taken him to the office and got the park people involved with finding his father. But, you know, what you did was better. You got Drew involved. He found his own dad. I doubt that he'll even remember this when he grows up. It's not going to leave a scar."

She got the implication. Drew wouldn't have a scar like hers. Referring to it directly felt like one of those things that would rouse emotions. Instead, she returned the favor and held a puff of the candy up to his mouth. He took it and then kissed her fingertips and looped his arm around her shoulders to pull her in close while the sugar dissolved.

"What other situations do you think might scare you? If I left you here and went home, what would you do?"

"Get a taxi, go home and kick you in the—"

He stopped her before she actually said the words by laying a hand over her mouth. "So you could handle that. What other situations do you get worried about in public places?" He slid his hand down to the side of her neck, where he could play with her hair and stroke her skin at the same time.

She lost the small amount of emotion that had come with her realization about her public fear, replaced by the warm, tingly feeling on her skin that came any time he played with her hair. "I...feel like I might not know what I'm supposed to do, and I'll do something wrong. Get into trouble, or make everyone hate me."

"That one I understand. I had it the first couple of years at school. But after I figured out the right comeback for some dude getting in my face and calling me a 'circus freak,' it stopped having any power over me. Different doesn't mean bad. Different is just different." And in a quieter voice he asked, "What did you do that was wrong when you were in the home?"

He would have to put that together. "I...drank out of the garden hose. I didn't know any of the cartoons the other kids knew. I kept asking where their horses were, and where we were going next... Different to kids is bad. Not just to them. It was all different than what I understood, and that confused me and upset me. A lot."

"How did you get your shoulder dislocated?" he asked, his voice so deceptively quiet that she almost missed that he'd linked it with her group home ordeal...

"You remembered..."

"Pink sling," he confirmed with two words.

What could she say about that? She still didn't know why it had happened. "I guess I made Mrs. Barch mad."

"Mrs. Barch?"

"She ran the home. But hated kids, near as I could tell." So naturally she'd made kids her career...

"What did you do to make her mad?" His hand slid into her hair, distracting her a little...probably distracting himself.

"I don't know. I know I say that when I don't want to talk about something, but I honestly don't know. I climbed onto the counter to reach the phone on the wall and the next I knew she jerked me down by the arm. I threw up on her. It really hurt. She sent me to bed for being bad. A couple of days later...Mom and Mack got there. The social worker gave them grief, I guess. Kids whose families aren't in the circus don't get abducted, I guess. But the instant Mom saw my arm, the social worker lady realized she'd put me with someone who'd do that...and then left it dislocated for days without taking me to the emergency room. She'd have gotten into trouble.

"So she sent me with Mom, and they were so glad to have me back they didn't file any complaints." It had taken Jolie most of her life to riddle out exactly what had happened with the social worker, the things you missed when you're little...

Reece scowled so hard Jolie was suddenly more than half-afraid he'd tell her to stop being dramatic or something else that made it her fault. But he let go of her hair, wrapped his arm around her shoulders and pulled her snugly against his side. The kiss he pressed to her temple lasted and lasted, and when he eventually spoke it was against her skin. "I should have asked what happened."

"You were eight." Jolie knew she might never learn to navigate the outside world but maybe she could learn to navigate this man. "You took good care of me. Everyone did. But you and Gordy especially."

He made a sound so contrary that Jolie tugged his head to hers to kiss him and subtly shift the conversation. "Thank you for going along with the shoulder thing. You know I was about a heartbeat away from climbing onto your shoulders."

"You know better than to think I couldn't have picked you up," he joked, but his voice said he was still upset.

"Oh, no I'm sure Strong Man could have, but Safety Man—you remember the other side of your personality? He would not have been very happy if I had. I didn't have any spotters, no safety gear on… What if you dropped me?"

"That's not how it goes and you know it." Reece goosed her ribs, and when she was giggling he stood, picked her up and tossed her over his shoulder.

She laughed and hit him on the butt. "Dirty! My defenses were down!" He didn't put her down, just started walking. "You know when you do these things in public, wearing that T-shirt, you're representing Keightly…" Right across the pavilion…in full view of the adults, who squinted, and the children, who laughed…off they went to the exit.

Jolie braced one arm against his back to hold herself up and waved her cotton candy at the kids they passed with the other so no one would be alarmed, and dropped the sugary stuff into a trashcan as they passed it. "Hey, Hercules, where are we going?"

"Home."

Thank God. And if he knew what was good for him, it had better be for sex.

The trapeze didn't smell like sawdust, but it had the same effect on Reece. He had thought the more he got up on the thing, the better he would do with it, but he still always felt on the edge of panic the whole time. His grim glowers even kind of scared the girls in the troupe. He needed to work on that but taking on one more thing seemed too much right now.

Every evening during the week, before the kids were picked up, Reece came and worked with them on the trapeze. The first two weeks of flying with a catcher, they'd all learned the knee-hang and how to fly back onto the swing when another girl swung out to meet them.

It took another two weeks for Reece's body to re-learn the ins and outs of the whole dangerous business, and for the old muscle memory to adjust to his new, bigger body. Only then did he feel comfortable adding the simple toss to their routine. The extra hour he spent teaching Anthony to catch in the evenings helped. Anthony taking the role was the light at the end of Reece's trapeze tunnel…

Two weeks later Reece added the simple toss to their routine. Things were going well.

With Reece's rigorous physicals and safety standards and Jolie's strict behavior policies it meant that at the rehearsal for the end-of-summer finale show they only had light injuries. The worst had come in the form of a scissor incident in costuming, and it had been when Reece hadn't been around and had only required a couple of stitches.

"How are you doing?" Jolie asked as he stretched his arms and shoulders, preparing to climb the ladder up to the platform.

He turned round so she could push his arm up from the back, stretching his shoulders better. "I'm fine. Have you decided if you're going to do anything during the finale?"

"I don't really want to. I don't want to show up the kids. They've been working hard all summer." She moved to the other arm, repeating the stretch he preferred.

He nodded, looking no less grim as he took to the ladder to get on with today's rehearsal.

Jolie moved off to the stands and took a seat, eyes fixed on the group above. They didn't need her direction today. She simply waited for Reece to climb on the screen and then pressed "Play' on the music that would accompany the aerial act.

The kids had gone for a haunted-circus theme, and every piece of music sounded like a deranged calliope, taking to the minor keys. While she really liked the theme the kids had put together all summer for the show, today, with Reece's mood, it put her on edge.

Anthony was the best at the knee-hang, but he really wanted Reece to be proud of him, Jolie could tell. He also was a little too confident for her liking. Two days ago Jolie had caught Anthony and his girlfriend, Tara, on the trapeze one evening after the camp was closed, practicing together. She'd put a stop to it. But she hadn't told Reece. He was so on edge about the trapeze already.

Reece got his swing where it needed to be, found his mark, and called, "Hep!" which got the first flyer launching on the swing.

He'd started self-medicating with anti-nausea medicine about three weeks ago, and he had been a little late taking them today because of a small emergency at the office. He wasn't sure he'd taken it in time to get the full effect, but the symptoms when he was in the air never started until he'd been at it for a few tricks and had had time to work himself into a mental lather.

It was psychosomatic, and he knew that Jolie would understand—she had waded through a few panic attacks this spring—but he didn't want her to know. It felt like breaking a promise to her if his mind was making him unable to complete the trapeze position he'd agreed to.

The first flier flew from the bar to his hands. Like always, she looked up at him nervously, like he was going to fling her off the swing. The three girls in the troupe always looked at him nervously. The only one who took every flight with extreme glee and confidence was Anthony—the fourth flier, it was a necessary part of learning to catch.

It would let the kids down if Reece couldn't catch. And the camp. Anthony just wasn't ready to do the catching yet but he got his shot earlier with the knee-hangs. He and Tara had worked that trick out very well during classes.

They each got a shot with the same tricks. The girls went, and when it was Anthony's turn Reece marked his swing and yelled, "Hep!" but noticed when he swung back toward his new younger brother that he was standing on the bar.

"Anthony!" he yelled. A combination of his lateness in taking the anti-nausea and vertigo pills and the surprise trick combined to rob him of the ability to say anything else. Anthony launched up at the wrong time, executed a perfect forward somersault, but when the timing was off, it didn't matter how perfect the trick was.

He was close. Reece stretched for Anthony's hands and only got one of them, throwing his swing off balance so that it swung on the diagonal.

Anthony seemed to understand only when their hands were slipping how dangerous what he'd done had been, and let go to let the net catch him.

The wrong point in the swing. The wrong time. Reece could do nothing but watch Anthony fall and pray he hit the net. They learned to fall properly the first day.

Anthony bounced once at the edge and then flew off into the ring.

Jolie had her phone out, dialing 911, before Anthony even let go of Reece's hand. But it all happened so fast. She ran with the phone to her ear, and gave report and instructions as she fell at Anthony's side.

"He's breathing," she called to Reece. And he, ever the protector, unfolded from the swing and fell to the net as soon as it was safe to do so, taking the fastest route down so he could get to them.

Breathing, but unconscious. She dared not move him, but reached to check his pulse, and breathed a tiny bit easier when she found a strong beat with her fingertips.

Reece knelt beside the unconscious teen and began checking for injuries. "More broken legs." His voice rasped. "Looks like the left tibia. Simple."

Jolie didn't even need to look at him to know how he was doing. His skin had turned ashen, but his hands were steady. This had to be like a nightmare for him.

Anthony started to wake up, and Reece found his voice. "*Do not move*, Anthony. You could have a neck or spine injury. I know you're in pain, but be still." And then added to Jolie, "Brace his head with your knees. Don't let him turn it."

He moved on from the obvious bones to Anthony's abdomen, prodding lightly as he watched the kid's face. "You tell me if this hurts, okay?" Jolie watched as well, as Reece's hands moved around Anthony's belly. At the left side, under the ribs, he pressed and Anthony cried out.

Reece stopped pressing, folded one of Anthony's arms up for Jolie to reach and said in tones so level and steady that her hair stood on end, "Keep an eye on his pulse. I need your phone."

"My pocket." She pressed Anthony's wrist, finding the pulse and counting the beats as she alternated between looking at her watch and watching Anthony's face.

Reece walked a short distance away and called, she assumed, 911 again. She heard the "words possible splenic rupture' and noticed that Anthony's pulse rate was increasing.

"Reece? His pulse is speeding up…a little."

He hung up and came back over. "How much?"

"What's happening?" Anthony asked, his voice breathy, scared.

Jolie answered Reece, frowning, "It's gone up from one-eighteen to one-twenty-five." And then said to the youngest Bohannon, "Do you hear the ambulance? Don't worry. Everything is going to be okay. The ambulance is here and we'll get you to the hospital and patched up. But you need to stay calm, okay?"

The paramedics stepped in, and with Reece's help got Anthony loaded onto a backboard and into the ambulance.

"Go with him," Jolie said to Reece, knowing he would be of assistance. "I'll be right behind you."

She should have told Reece that she'd found them practicing. Tara had gotten the message that she could be kicked out of the camp and not allowed back next year for the stunt with the trapeze, but Anthony had had something to prove. And he'd wanted to impress Reece more than anyone. If she'd told Reece, he could have gotten through to Anthony.

This was her fault.

But Reece would blame himself.

Six hours later Reece had yet to speak to Jolie. She moved along beside him through the hospital, everywhere she could go. He was a doctor so they let him into Recovery to see Anthony when he came out of surgery. And he left Jolie in the waiting room with every single person who lived at the farm—even Granny and the brood of young wild things she fostered.

He just couldn't think about her right now or how she'd take it when he told her the camp was done. No more. No show. No next season. Anthony could have died. But, really, any of them could have died. It didn't matter how safe they played it, when it came time for that last show, the safety gear came off. And he'd fallen for it—the idea that these were safe tricks. That this was fine. He should have been listening to his gut when every time he'd got into the swing, he'd almost thrown up.

Reece stayed back with Anthony as they removed the tube in his throat and Reece got to talk to him.

"You know I'm going to kick your ass when you get better," Reece said, taking Anthony's hand and leaning over the bed so he could look him in the eye.

Anthony smiled, and Reece relaxed.

"I thought you'd catch me."

Reece shook his head, but he was so relieved he couldn't do anything but rib him. "I would have if you had told me what you were going to do. But you're lucky. Your spleen ruptured, but they got it out clean. You survived a ruptured spleen, which is fairly badass. You also have a broken leg, and it's a simple fracture. Granny wanted them to put you in a pink cast with flowers, but I intervened. That old lady is so upset she's forgotten how to swear."

"Sign of the apocalypse, isn't it?"

"Sources say." Reece grinned and then did something that probably would have horrified the kid if he wasn't drugged, and especially if chicks were watching. He dropped a kiss on Anthony's head. "We want you around until you're old enough to cuss like Granny Bohannon.

You don't need to impress anyone, you already have. And if you don't believe how many people love you, when they wheel you to your room, I want you to look at the waiting room."

Anthony's eyes squeezed shut and a couple of tears slipped out, but he nodded. "Thanks, Reece."

Reece squeezed his hand.

"If you tell anyone I cried, I'm going to tell them you kissed me."

Reece smirked and let go. "All right, Spleeny." He made his farewells before the recovery nurses kicked him out, and went out to speak with the family.

Later that evening, when the hospital administration made it clear that visiting hours were over, Jolie waited for everyone to exit Anthony's room and then went to speak with him. Luckily, she found him in one of his post-surgery lucid phases and took his hand. "We're going to head home, but Granny is going to be here bright and early in the morning to sit with you. Do you want one of us to stay here with you tonight?"

Anthony smiled a little and shook his head. "I'm okay. Could you call Tara for me?"

"She's been here, honey," Jolie told him, grinning. "And her parents just dragged her home a few minutes ago. But you were sleeping. She knows you're going to be okay. She'll probably bring you something she baked tomorrow...and yell at you."

"Doesn't do any good," he muttered.

Jolie knew precisely what he was talking about: her yelling at him. "Well, it would have been better if you hadn't needed to learn the hard way, but you came through it. Everyone's going to be fine."

"Reece isn't. He's...very upset still."

"Reece learned his lesson the hard way once already."

Again she wished she'd just told him about Anthony and Tara. It was her fault really that Anthony was hurt. She was too lenient...or maybe not intimidating enough. Something. She should have handled something differently.

"His dad," Anthony filled in.

"His dad."

"No one will tell me how it happened."

No one liked to talk about it. Jolie didn't like to talk about it, but maybe if she had used it to scare him the other day this wouldn't have happened. Not talking about things wasn't working out for her on so many levels.

"It was equipment malfunction, a Russian swing. His dad was flying on that one. They take two fliers to get the swing moving fast and high enough, and then the front person lets go and kind of...catapults really fast and far to the catcher. Much further than regular catches." She tried to explain gently and quickly, knowing he needed his rest.

Anthony squeezed her hand. "Something broke?"

"Reece was the additional power on the swing. He wasn't supposed to fly, just be at the back to get it going, and he's really good at that. Has a powerful swing." She had to stop and focus on something to keep the mental images away. "Whoever installed it the last time hadn't done a good job. One of the bolts had stripped and as there were a number of other bolts, he'd just figured he'd change it the next time it was set up."

"Did it break?" Anthony asked, the horror in his voice pulling her attention back to his bruised face.

She nodded. "Before his dad jumped, the swing came loose...at the worst time...and they both pitched off it at a really bad angle, moving fast. It looked like they were both going to miss the net, but somehow only Henry missed it. Reece hit it. I think Henry pushed him or flung him off course somehow. He had the air knocked out of him but his dad hit the rigging and then the ground. He didn't die instantly. There was so much blood...and the EMTs didn't get there in time." Which was why Jolie had studied emergency medicine and was a certified EMT.

It had been so long since she'd even let herself remember it...

"So he checks the rigging every day," Anthony supplied.

"I don't know how to make him stop or even if I should try," Jolie confirmed. "Anyway, he's not mad at you, but he might ride you when you get out of this antiseptic-smelling lock-up, but it's just because he's feeling really protective of you."

Anthony nodded. She squeezed his hand again. "We all are. Now sleep. I'm sure Granny will bring you something in the morning to keep you amused. Or maybe she'll make you write 'I will not pull unexpected tricks on the trapeze' one thousand times. Either way, rest." She leaned up and in to reach his cheek, kissed it, and then went to find Reece.

Jolie walked with Reece to the garage. "We should talk about this..." she said, hurrying to keep up with his longer stride. She wanted to hold his hand, but he had them crammed into his pockets.

"When we get back to the farm."

He knew. He knew and he thought she was an utter failure as a camp director.

The trip home felt like a drive to her execution.

Jolie just wasn't sure whether it was the end of them or the end of the camp.

CHAPTER ELEVEN

JOLIE STOPPED THE car and Reece climbed out and set off for the big top. "Reece, you don't need to go back in there right now."

"I have to," Reece bit out, not looking back at her. "I'm taking down the trapeze."

She ran to cover the distance being eaten up by his long stride and grabbed his hand. "I already locked up the ladders. No one can get up to there without getting the ladders unlocked."

He scowled but stopped and looked back at her. "I'll check. Go to your trailer and wait."

As much as she wanted to make him stop and listen to her, talk to her, just be with her until she knew he was okay, Jolie let go of his hand and did as he requested.

She almost hoped Anthony had told him then at least he'd place the blame on her—where it belonged—not blame himself.

After she reached the trailer and got inside, she stepped back out where she could best see the tent and waited for Reece to arrive.

And when he still hadn't come half an hour later she sat on the stairs and waited.

The good news was that she could now unequivocally say that she had control of her emotions again. Calm. She'd managed to stay calm through the whole thing. Right now she was worried but able to keep the panic at bay.

She folded her arms on her knees and laid her head down, giving him the time he needed despite her natural inclination to run after him.

Reece had to admire Jolie's simple solution to lock up the ladders. She'd climbed them and pulled the tail of the rope ladder up behind her. They draped over the platforms, where no one could get to them without extreme effort and construction ladders locked up in the pole barn.

Checking her solution had taken about a minute, and then he spent the next forty minutes throwing up.

Jolie had gone to her trailer, as he'd asked. He saw she was sitting on the stairs with her head on her knees, waiting for him. Hearing his approach, she lifted her head. "You look like hell."

"Yeah. I need a drink," Reece muttered.

She stood, heading into her home to get him a glass of water. "Or did you mean booze?"

He took the glass and drank it all. When it was empty and his mouth was a little improved, he looked at her. "The camp is over, Jo. No finale show. No camp next year. I'm going to call up the buyer from this spring and see if his offer is still on the table."

The calm with which she took his ruling seemed off. She held out a hand for the glass and took it back to the kitchen. "Are you okay?"

"I'm... No." He may as well tell her. "I've been—"

"It was my fault that he did that," she said quietly, stopping him in his tracks.

Reece turned and sat on the couch, taking up entirely too much room in the small home when he stood around in it. "What do you mean?"

"I caught him and Tara on the trapeze the other evening, and I chewed them both out." Her voice was level, no tears in sight, though she looked haunted by guilt, and there was a small tell about how upset it had made her in the way she kept holding her own hands. "I got through to Tara, but I guess I didn't get through to Anthony. And I didn't tell you because I didn't want you to be upset. I thought I'd handled it...but I hadn't. If it had come from you, he would have listened."

"He might have," Reece said, but shrugged. "Hard to say. It was probably a matter of time. And, really, we're lucky it was family. If it had been one of the kids, they could have sued."

She finally moved to the couch and sat beside him. "Next year—"

"There won't be a next year, Jolie." He needed to stand. She was too close and when she was close he wanted to please and protect her, physically and emotionally. Best she stayed outside arm's reach. "This life is too dangerous. And you're not performing because of it as I thought you would. You teach, and your students are doing great on the wire, but you're not performing except those times you practice your routine, which I thought you were going to perform at the finale, but you said no. So what's the point?"

He turned back to look at her on the couch, silent and frowning. Was it because she worried about him or she was trying to work out how to make him do what she wanted? He didn't know.

"Where does this leave us?"

She probably wouldn't want to wait for a solution to appear, or like the solution he had in mind. "I love you, Jo. But there's no future for us if you're on the road, and there's no happiness for you if you're not in the life. And

I don't even know if I could handle it if you were performing. We tried to preserve the life with the camp, but it can't work. So you tell me, what's the solution? Do you want to come and work at my practice? Make appointments and sit all day at a desk? Good Lord, you're like the ultimate riddle."

"Once again, I am a problem to be solved."

"Stop saying that."

Naturally, he would wait until he could couch it in break-up words before he said "I love you' the first time.

"Sounds like you have made up your mind."

"I have to protect you." He said the words softly, but they may as well have been shouted.

Jolie shook her head. "I'm not your responsibility."

"Yes, you are my responsibility." He laughed, a short, mirthless sound. "And I know how stupid that sounds when I say it out loud, but I'm supposed to protect you. I'm still on that job."

"The job your dad gave you when I was five?" What could she say to that? He'd all but admitted it was insane.

He plowed his hand through his hair. "Yes."

"Is that why you love me? Because I'm your responsibility to take care of?"

"No. That's why I try so hard not to love you. Makes it that much harder to take care of you properly when every time you're sad it's a lance through my chest." He stepped to the door, ready to escape. "I have a list of owners who are looking for a wire act. I'll send it over tomorrow. Email."

"You've been...you've been headhunting a job for me?" She didn't know whether to cry or scream.

"I was just getting a feel for whether there was a market."

"How long? Recently? All summer? When did you take

this little task on your shoulders?" She rubbed between her brows. Some of that old numbness began seeping in and she let it. "You know what? Never mind. I don't want either of us to say anything else. Something we might regret. We'll talk again when we have clear heads."

"My head is clear, honey."

"Are you blaming yourself?"

"I'm blaming everyone. You. Me. Anthony. The people in his past who made that kid feel like even when he was part of a family he had to keep working to make them love him. And I'm blaming the lure of the big top and the thrill of flying." He opened the door and stepped out. "I'll talk to you soon."

At least that would be different this time. He didn't want to hurt her, but he would be man enough to put it to her straight before he left her.

Reece drove his car through the grass to park on the far side of the big top, and he didn't care who didn't like it. There was a trail of dust streaking across the flat Georgia landscape where he'd raced down the long dusty drive. At least driving on the grass wouldn't make life difficult for any asthmatics on the farm.

He wouldn't have had to do this if the whole area hadn't been packed with cars and fans—spectators, he imagined.

Jolie had called that morning and left a message that the season finale recital of Keightly Circus Camp would be going ahead, and had then refused to answer any of his calls when he rang her back.

Inside the tent, all the seating had been installed and it was packed to the gills with people. He saw all manner of dressed performers below the stands, which traditionally served as the backstage area for performers about to come out.

It wasn't a haunted circus. It was a zombie circus.

But no matter how cute it was, it could not go on. "Anyone seen Miss Jolie?" he asked, making the circuit around the tent via that backstage portion. Children pointed in the direction he traveled, and he eventually found her counting heads. Without saying anything to alert the kids, he grabbed her elbow and steered her out of the tent, where he might possibly choke her to death. "Call it off."

"Reece, just listen. There is no trapeze act. These kids have worked too hard to miss their finale. However, all the safety equipment is being used. And you're just going to have to trust me. I know I screwed up with Anthony, but don't take it out on the kids. They need this. They deserve it."

He looked toward the flap and a bizarre little grey-skinned hobo clown smiled at him. And waved. Reece waved back at the little boy then looked at Jolie. "You should have told me."

"Yes. I should have. There's a lot of things I should have told you. And when you said you loved me, even though you said it under duress, I should have believed you."

"You didn't believe me?"

"Not until later." She touched his face and then pressed her thumb between his brows and gave the muscle a little rub. It actually felt good, forcing his brow to relax. "I promise we've taken every precaution that's possible. I know you'll approve of what we've done. It's more camp than circus now. And the only way someone's going to get hurt is if a meteor falls. No trapeze. Please, Reece. Just go and watch the show. I saved you a seat by Granny." She turned to head for the tent again.

"What about the aerialists?"

"They have a new act." She stopped before entering. "And they've worked like crazy the past week to get it ready. It's not on the trapeze. And it doesn't even need a net. Okay?"

He was holding up the show. Reece sighed and walked inside. Once again he'd failed to say no to Jolie. Finding Granny easily enough, he took a seat and tried to relax. Mouth like a sailor and a heart of gold, she laid a weathered hand over his and gave him a comforting pat. "Don't worry, everything's gonna be okay."

"I hope so."

He must have looked sick because she let go of his hand, reached for her purse and put it in his lap. "But if you have to throw up, there's a barf bag in there. I stole it from the hospital." When he didn't say anything, she added, "Them zombies are disgusting."

Over the next two hours he watched the most ridiculously cute zombie-clown parody since the *Thriller* video that he had to laugh. They always started with the clowns.

Then came jugglers with fake bones, balls painted with skulls, sticks modeled like femurs...

Stiff-legged acrobats, who shuffled around before breaking into feats of creepy, contorted tumbling.

And toward the end an oddly placed fashion show where the kid designers talked about the costuming. While the little zombie fashion show was going on, the crew went about in the background, setting something up.

Thick mats went down. Cables suspended from the rigging high above were brought down to dangle and large steel hoops were attached to the ends. Set in the wide shape of a square, so all around the tent everyone would have a good view.

Then he saw his aerialists, minus Anthony, walking out in single file, dressed all in black with gauzy fabric tatters hanging everywhere. While the rest of the show had pre-recorded music with it, he heard the first strains of the calliope as the girls took their positions in the hoops. Mack drove the calliope into the ring with his mother at the keyboard, playing what he could only call music of a haunted carousel.

The stage hands got the hoops spinning. He'd made sure all the trapeze troupe had been gymnasts...except Anthony. Give a gymnast a big spinning hoop to play with? They probably liked it just as well as the trapeze, and at only three feet from thick mats Jolie was right, it would be a miracle if they found a way to hurt themselves badly.

They found artistic ways to arrange themselves within the hoops, each move slowing or increasing the speed of the spin. It was flashy and graceful, and a little bit creepy with the calliope. And as he watched, he forgot the horror that always darkened his circus experience.

Jolie had done it. They'd got off to a rocky start but next year there would be a waiting list a mile long to come to the camp. At the end she made a short speech, giving recognition to all of the former Keightly Circus performers and especially to him, who...

He could fill in that blank. Reece, who had made her beg and plead to be allowed to try it. Reece, who treated her like an incompetent child. Reece, who left for long stretches of time because he couldn't control everyone.

Not that she said any of that. He waved his hand at the applause and circulated through the crowd of parents and performers, giving his congratulations. Then he went to Jolie's trailer to wait for her. She'd left the door unlocked, as usual, so when she finally got back she found him sitting on her stairs with a glass of tea in his hand. The problem was, no matter how long he'd sat there, he didn't know what to say to her. His feelings were all still scrambled in his head.

* * *

"You were right. I didn't see anything there that...wasn't amazing. And the kids deserved their shot to do the show. I hope someone taped the zombie clown *Thriller* dance."

Jolie smiled and came to a stop in front of the stairs, just far away that he couldn't touch her without standing up. "Oh, don't worry, we have the whole thing on tape. It might be one of a kind. Collector's edition."

"About that..." Reece licked his lips. "About next year..."

"Wait. I want to talk about us. Can we talk about us first?" She stepped closer, her courage faltering a little. He'd been smiling at the circus. He'd enjoyed it. She should have stuck with that topic. She could handle that topic...

Reece tilted his head back toward the living room. "Do you want to come inside to do this?"

"No. With you on the stairs, we're closer to the same eye level right now. The height changes inside, nothing that tall for you to sit on," Jolie babbled, then paused, took a breath to find her center again and started over. "I have a speech. And if we go moving around, I might forget it. Or forget how it starts."

"You have a speech?" Reece reached behind him to set the glass of tea inside then focused on her. "I'm ready."

"You said I didn't trust you, and you were right. I didn't. I wanted to, and I tried. I knew you were trying. But it just wasn't coming together for me. When I got on the trapeze with you that day, I couldn't bring myself to reach for you. When we did the knee-hang, it was different. I never had to let go of the bar until you had hold of me securely. But when we did the toss and I had to let go of the bar, I couldn't take your hands, even when they were a sure thing. Not because I thought I would fall, I thought it was possible that you would drop me. And just that possibility seemed so much worse than me deciding to fall on my own. It doesn't make a lot of sense."

Reece waved a hand. "It does. That was about being in control, even if the decision you made was one that could have hurt you. I understand that need for control. Believe me." He was very calm. If that meant he didn't care, he was going to have to reject her twice, because she wasn't going to stop.

"I don't even know when I started to trust you. It wasn't like there was a light-bulb moment when I thought, Everything's okay, I can trust Reece now. He hasn't broken his promises or whatever. The whole summer, and even when we got back from the hospital and...well, we broke up, right? I expected it. I had been waiting for it the whole summer. And then you had that list, and it seemed like you had been expecting it too." She felt tears burning her eyes and had to stop talking for a moment to breathe.

"I could be a total psycho and ask you to get on the trapeze to prove to you that I trust you, but I don't need to do that. I already reached for you...today. I knew you would be mad about the show, but I knew you would come. I know you'll always come, Reece. I know it. Even if you..." Her voice cracked and she squeaked the rest in the most undignified fashion while swiping her cheeks. "Even if you don't want me any more."

He stood, took two steps toward her, reached out, and his hands didn't close. "Are you done with your speech?"

She nodded.

His arms surged around her waist and he picked her up, carried her inside, his mouth on hers before the door closed, and her pants were off before they got to the bed.

Ten minutes later Reece rolled onto his back, dragging her with him. "Sorry. I meant to last and last..."

"It was longer than five seconds," she teased, smiling.

He groaned, "I'm never going to live that one down, am I?"

She scooted up closer so she could tuck her nose beneath his chin. "You do every time. I just like to make sure you don't lose the magic." And then she pulled back to look him in the eye. "And you had it at the show tonight, didn't you? Not the sexy magic, but...you felt it, didn't you?"

"I forgot where I was, who I was...and why I had left. That's the first time that's happened. Yes." He pushed her hair back from her face. "I felt the magic. If you want the camp next year, I'm good with that. I think if you run it like you have done this year—"

"Without the trapeze," Jolie cut in.

He smiled, looking relieved. "Without the trapeze. The hoops were wonderful. I'd rather you stay away from the silk aerialists, though. That's more dangerous than trapeze."

"I agree." She kissed him again and said, "We don't have to make any decisions. I don't want to travel, but I did find out that I can get an agent to arrange corporate gigs and big parties, short-term travel if I do feel like performing. But, honestly, the idea of having a pasture to ride in every day, maybe get a miniature mare and breed them? One day build a house with a foundation? That idea's starting to grow on me. I still don't think I could handle suburbia but...I can handle not traveling. I can make a life, a happy life, outside The Life."

"You work on building a life outside The Life, I'll work on making sure it's happy." Reece didn't propose, but it was as good as she needed.

She sat up, straddling his groin, and gave a slow wiggle. "I owe you an 'I love you.' I'll see if I can find one lying about if you can last longer than ten minutes this time."

"If I can't, I'm sure we can find Mr. Happy around

here somewhere..." he said, rolling her over and kissing her breathless.

Strides may have been made today, but the man still liked to be in charge.

And that was okay. Jolie knew she had all the time in the world to break him of it.

* * * * *

Mills & Boon® Hardback

August 2014

ROMANCE

Zarif's Convenient Queen	Lynne Graham
Uncovering Her Nine Month Secret	Jennie Lucas
His Forbidden Diamond	Susan Stephens
Undone by the Sultan's Touch	Caitlin Crews
The Argentinian's Demand	Cathy Williams
Taming the Notorious Sicilian	Michelle Smart
The Ultimate Seduction	Dani Collins
Billionaire's Secret	Chantelle Shaw
The Heat of the Night	Amy Andrews
The Morning After the Night Before	Nikki Logan
Here Comes the Bridesmaid	Avril Tremayne
How to Bag a Billionaire	Nina Milne
The Rebel and the Heiress	Michelle Douglas
Not Just a Convenient Marriage	Lucy Gordon
A Groom Worth Waiting For	Sophie Pembroke
Crown Prince, Pregnant Bride	Kate Hardy
Daring to Date Her Boss	Joanna Neil
A Doctor to Heal Her Heart	Annie Claydon

MEDICAL

Tempted by Her Boss	Scarlet Wilson
His Girl From Nowhere	Tina Beckett
Falling For Dr Dimitriou	Anne Fraser
Return of Dr Irresistible	Amalie Berlin

ROMANCE

A D'Angelo Like No Other	Carole Mortimer
Seduced by the Sultan	Sharon Kendrick
When Christakos Meets His Match	Abby Green
The Purest of Diamonds?	Susan Stephens
Secrets of a Bollywood Marriage	Susanna Carr
What the Greek's Money Can't Buy	Maya Blake
The Last Prince of Dahaar	Tara Pammi
The Secret Ingredient	Nina Harrington
Stolen Kiss From a Prince	Teresa Carpenter
Behind the Film Star's Smile	Kate Hardy
The Return of Mrs Jones	Jessica Gilmore

HISTORICAL

Unlacing Lady Thea	Louise Allen
The Wedding Ring Quest	Carla Kelly
London's Most Wanted Rake	Bronwyn Scott
Scandal at Greystone Manor	Mary Nichols
Rescued from Ruin	Georgie Lee

MEDICAL

Tempted by Dr Morales	Carol Marinelli
The Accidental Romeo	Carol Marinelli
The Honourable Army Doc	Emily Forbes
A Doctor to Remember	Joanna Neil
Melting the Ice Queen's Heart	Amy Ruttan
Resisting Her Ex's Touch	Amber McKenzie

Mills & Boon® Hardback
September 2014

ROMANCE

The Housekeeper's Awakening	Sharon Kendrick
More Precious than a Crown	Carol Marinelli
Captured by the Sheikh	Kate Hewitt
A Night in the Prince's Bed	Chantelle Shaw
Damaso Claims His Heir	Annie West
Changing Constantinou's Game	Jennifer Hayward
The Ultimate Revenge	Victoria Parker
Tycoon's Temptation	Trish Morey
The Party Dare	Anne Oliver
Sleeping with the Soldier	Charlotte Phillips
All's Fair in Lust & War	Amber Page
Dressed to Thrill	Bella Frances
Interview with a Tycoon	Cara Colter
Her Boss by Arrangement	Teresa Carpenter
In Her Rival's Arms	Alison Roberts
Frozen Heart, Melting Kiss	Ellie Darkins
After One Forbidden Night...	Amber McKenzie
Dr Perfect on Her Doorstep	Lucy Clark

MEDICAL

A Secret Shared...	Marion Lennox
Flirting with the Doc of Her Dreams	Janice Lynn
The Doctor Who Made Her Love Again	Susan Carlisle
The Maverick Who Ruled Her Heart	Susan Carlisle

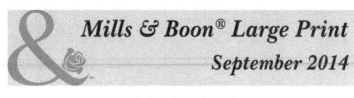

Mills & Boon® Large Print

September 2014

ROMANCE

HISTORICAL

MEDICAL

0814 GEN STD LP

MILLS & BOON®

Why shop at millsandboon.co.uk?

Each year, thousands of romance readers find their perfect read at millsandboon.co.uk. That's because we're passionate about bringing you the very best romantic fiction. Here are some of the advantages of shopping at www.millsandboon.co.uk:

* **Get new books first**—you'll be able to buy your favourite books one month before they hit the shops

* **Get exclusive discounts**—you'll also be able to buy our specially created monthly collections, with up to 50% off the RRP

* **Find your favourite authors**—latest news, interviews and new releases for all your favourite authors and series on our website, plus ideas for what to try next

* **Join in**—once you've bought your favourite books, don't forget to register with us to rate, review and join in the discussions

Visit **www.millsandboon.co.uk**
for all this and more today!